LOVE UNDER THE SPOTLIGHT

PRASANNA RATANJANKAR

INDIA • SINGAPORE • MALAYSIA

Chapter 1

"Zeshan *Bhai* (brother), *ikde ikde* (this way)!"

"Right Bhai, look right!"

"Zeshan, straight, Bhai straight!"

"Bhai, cheese!"

FLASH!

Zeshan's heart raced with excitement as he leaned against the fancy front gate of St. Vincent's, the super cool academy full of secrets and dreams. He had this expensive designer backpack slung over his shoulder, and his shades made him look all mysterious. The sunlight sparkled on his glasses, and everyone was taking his picture with their cameras. It felt like a movie moment, just on an ordinary day.

His outfit was cool but casual. He had on a crisp white t-shirt that fit him perfectly and jeans that had seen their fair share of adventures. The star of the show, though, was his bomber jacket. Even though it was hot and humid in June in Mumbai, Zeshan wore it with style, like it was made just for him.

A little breeze messed up his hair, but when he posed, he looked confident and ready for big dreams. The world around him faded away, and he was like the main character in his own story, the one everyone wanted to take pictures of.

But the secret to his fame was a girl named Jigna Patel, his behind-the-scenes fairy godmother. She was sneaky and sent messages to the paparazzi on WhatsApp to tell them where Zeshan was. She helped make every camera click sound like a love song, turning him into a star in pictures and stories.

With all the fame and camera flashes, Zeshan stayed cool. He was like a prince in front of the adoring fans and the hot sun, ready to write his own story of love, dreams, and the magic hidden in every outfit he chose and every secret he whispered.

"Enough guys! It's my first day of college. I don't want to be late!"

"Zeshan, Zeshan, one last photo!"

How could he say no to that? He found himself striking a pose once again, ensuring the paparazzi captured that irresistible dimpled smile capable of setting countless teenage hearts aflutter. Those very teenagers had now swarmed the entrance, all eager for a glimpse of the one and only Zeshan Kapoor, the dazzling scion of Bollywood royalty, Raghav and Adhira Kapoor. Zeshan, in his charismatic fashion, gazed in the direction of his devoted female admirers, punctuating the scene with a sly wink, inciting a symphony of ecstatic, high-pitched screams that only heightened the pandemonium. Naturally, Zeshan reveled in every moment of it.

Zeel, on the other hand, had been patiently waiting in the car so far for her brother to get done with this circus. But now, her patience was wearing thin. She looked at her watch once again to see that they were, indeed, going to be late on their first day of college.

"Great," Zeel cursed the universe for giving her the one thing she could have actually done without - a Bollywood-nepo-baby for a twin brother! After all, she was the one person in the Kapoor *khaandaan* (family) who saw what the world of glitz and glamour was all about - lies, lies, and more lies!

The very media outlets that currently showered Zeshan with adoration had, merely a year ago, unleashed a relentless onslaught against her family. They had cast a shadow of disgrace over her older sister Zinia when she became embroiled in a scandal. The very paparazzi who now hung on Zeshan's every smile had descended upon her family like vultures, capturing her father's illicit rendezvous with a mistress half his age in the dimly lit alley behind The Taj Mahal Hotel. And the same fans who were swooning at Zeshan's wink would make it a point to send nasty DMs to Zeel on social media platforms criticizing her for everything from her dietary choices to her fashion sense.

While Zeel understood that Zeshan had to entertain fans and media given that he was being groomed to become the next superstar, she still couldn't understand how he had the stomach to stand there and smile as if everything was hunky dory in their lives. Guess her brother really was good at acting. If his performance in front of the paps right now was anything to go by, Zeshan would have the audience eating out of his hands the moment he debuted on the big screen.

Zeel let out a long sigh and finally got out of the car. She hated stepping in front of the paparazzi. Luckily for her, the media didn't like her much either. As one particularly bitchy gossip site had stated, "Zeel's entire personality could be summed up as a piece of soggy cardboard." While Zeel wasn't exactly sure what the 'journalist' had meant by that, it didn't really bother her.

Zeel didn't care about what the world thought about her. Neither did she care about her looks too much. She was pretty, she knew that much, but she didn't make it her whole personality. She had big, beautiful eyes framed by oversized glasses with a bright pink frame, lustrous dark long hair, and a lovely dusky complexion that she had inherited from her mother. However, early on in life, seeing her mother and then her sister obsessing over their looks and what the world thought about them made Zeel realize that she wanted to…no, needed to…focus on other things in life. This is why instead of spending hours at the salon, Zeel chose to hang out at bookstores, and instead of obsessing over boys at her school, Zeel obsessed over fictional hotties. She was content keeping her nose in a book and herself out of trouble.

As long as the hyenas left her alone, she couldn't care less what they said about her. Elbowing her way through the adoring fans and jumble of cameras, Zeel finally reached her brother. Grabbing him by the arm, she tried to pull him towards the gate.

"Let's go, Zishu! We're late!"

"*Aye kya re Zeel, hamesha maza kharaab karne aa jati hai* (Why do you always have to ruin the fun, Zeel?)," bellowed a particularly smarmy-eyed photographer.

Zeel shot him a venomous glance before turning to her brother, "Are you done? I don't want to be late because of you! How much longer are you going to pose?"

"Chill Zee! You know this is important," Zeshan said through clenched teeth while continuing to smile for the cameras.

"Dude, seriously?!"

"Oh, come on Zee! It's not like they're going to be here every day!" Her brother, who was enjoying the media attention a little too much, was clearly in no mood to make a move.

Zeel was just about getting ready to launch into a verbal attack on her brother when suddenly she saw the media being parted by two burly guards making way for none other than Principal Chitre who currently wore a look of murderous rage on her fifty-something face. Yup, that was all she needed for the day to go from bad to worse. Now they had gone and angered the college principal. All before even setting foot inside the college.

Principal Chitre strode straight toward the Kapoor siblings and demanded, "Mr. and Ms. Kapoor, why are you not in class yet? You're late for the first-year orientation."

Principal Manjiri Chitre's booming voice had managed to get the fangirls to scurry away like little rats abandoning a sinking ship. The paparazzi though were a tough crowd. One angry principal was nothing compared to the drama they were used to witnessing day in and day out. The scene unfolding in front of them was exactly the kind of non-sensical gossip that made headlines and Zeshan Kapoor, famous for doing absolutely nothing. Zeel couldn't help but roll her eyes while simultaneously being both furious with her brother and terrified of Principal Chitre's ire.

Before Zeel could answer the question, Principal Chitre continued, "Mr. Kapoor, please ask your media friends to leave. This is an educational institution, not your father's film studio! And Ms. Kapoor, I would have expected at least you to not partake in this media circus. Just because you were a topper in Junior College, don't think you can take it easy now!"

"Yes, ma'am. I completely understand…this won't happen again," Zeel found herself stuttering an apology even though she wasn't at fault.

Zeshan, on the other hand, was not even attempting to give Principal Chitre a half-assed sorry for all the trouble he had caused. But he did finally wave the paps goodbye, much to the chagrin of his publicist Jigna who rolled her eyes and led the last of the photographers away from Zeshan.

Within minutes, the media had melted away from the gates of St. Vincent's leaving Zeel and Zeshan in the presence of the still very angry Manjiri Chitre. However, before she could launch into yet another lecture about how they were being bad students, her attention was diverted to her phone which had started ringing rather loudly. Giving them one last look of disgust, Principal Chitre answered the call with a very interesting tone filled with resignment and a tinge of disdain, "What now, Tawde Sir? There are first-year students still milling about outside college. Weren't you supposed to begin the orientation ten minutes ago?"

Upon seeing the principal being caught up in scolding the vice-principal of the college, Zeshan took his chance and discretely steered Zeel toward the entrance. Putting his arm around his sister, he said, "See, it wasn't that bad, Zee. You know the old bat is famous for not letting students have any fun. I feel sorry for her kids, man. I've heard she's a total hard-ass when it comes to them. You know her son used to study here, the cricketer - Atharva Chitre? I've heard she was brutal with him. I've heard her daughter's studying here too. Won't be surprised if she gets her kids to join here just to be able to keep an eye on them!"

"How do you know all this?" Zeel was surprised at the level of her brother's knowledge regarding such things. She would have thought someone like Zeshan who attended college only to pass the time until his big on-screen debut, wouldn't be interested in all these things.

"I have my sources. Also, I believe in keeping tabs on my enemy's weaknesses dear sister. Unlike you who just dissolved into a blubbering mess in front of that cow, I actually have an entire strategy laid out to make sure she doesn't become a pain in my ass this year. I really don't want another suspension like I got in Junior College last year or Dad really will have my hide this time!"

Despite all his shenanigans, Zeshan really idolised their father and always strived to be in his good books. Which was yet another thing Zeel couldn't understand about her brother. How could she have shared a womb with this kid who idolized an adulterer was beyond her. But then again, it's not like she had any other solid role models to look up to either. On one hand was her father, 90s heartthrob, Raghav Kapoor who was currently shacked up with his 20-something girlfriend, and on the other hand was her mother who chose to drown her sorrows in a bottle of wine and regularly made a spectacle of herself at Bollywood parties.

Zeel pushed her brother away and started walking briskly towards her classroom, "I don't know why you care so much about what dad will do. In case you haven't noticed, he doesn't live with us anymore."

"Yeah well, I don't care what problems he's having with mom. But seriously, I need him, Zee. It would be best if he launches me in his next movie. If not, I could at least do with some good recommendations from him," said Zeshan.

Rolling her eyes for the umpteenth time, Zeel walked into the classroom. Eager to change the subject turning one last time to face her brother she said, "Thanks for nothing Zishu. Because of you, Principal Chitre thinks I'm not serious about my studies. I have a reputation to uphold dude!"

Zeshan let out a rather loud chortle at that, "Reputation? Zee, it's called being a NERD. That is not a reputation. That's the opposite of it!"

"Better a nerd than a psycho like you! How can you stand those paps, Zishu? They seem so fake!"

"They seem fake only to you Zee. To me, they're a vital ingredient that's going to make or break my career as an actor. So, suck it up and hang back while I pose for the pictures, or figure out a way to take the bus to college because guess what? These guys are absolutely going to be here every day, as long as I attend college."

Letting out an irritated "Aargh!" Zeel made her way to class, a chuckling Zeshan in tow.

***

"Zee! This way!"

Zeel could hear her friend Madiha call out to her. But finding her in the auditorium-style classroom was going to take a little more looking around.

"Zee, Maddy's sitting there," Zeshan pointed to the far left of the class, to a short girl with a heart-shaped face framed with lovely dark curls. Madiha was wearing a bright yellow top and baggy jeans and was furiously waving her hands to catch Zeel's attention. Her huge earrings…was she wearing flamingos in her ears?…were swinging wildly as she bounced on her seat.

Maddy, or Madiha Khan, had been Zeel's friend since they were in kindergarten. Madiha came from a big boisterous family that owned the real estate company, Khan Developments. Although she lost her parents to an accident when she was still a baby, Madiha never felt like she was alone because of her big fat joint family that consisted of two uncles, their wives, five cousins, an aunt, her grandparents, two sisters-in-law, three nieces, and nephews…you get the picture. Hence, every time she craved a moment to herself, she would make a beeline for Zee's house where she could be by herself…and secretly watch Zeshan whom she was absolutely not obsessed with!

"Yo Madz, whaddup!" Zeshan flounced down next to Madiha and planted a quick kiss on her cheek which turned her face the same colour as her flamingo earrings. "Thanks for saving me a seat!"

"The seat's not for you, you toad. Now let go of Maddy and go find your little fiefdom of fangirls to rule over somewhere else," said Zeel, shooing her brother away before giving Madiha a quick hug and setting her things down next to her, waiting for Zeshan to vacate the seat.

Zeshan shot his sister a dirty look and turned to give Madiha a quick wink, which somehow managed to redden her cheeks further before getting up and backing away from the seats. He had already scoped out the room and spotted his friend Raunak Khanna at the other end of the room and decided to make his way toward him, leaving of course a tide of sighing teenage girls in his wake. Raunak was yet another star-kid so to speak. Only his father Ajay Khanna wasn't an actor but a big Bollywood producer. Raunak was a good guy, but he had dropped out of college for a couple of years to work on a script he was developing, or that's what he had told everyone. He should have been graduating this year but instead here he was, stuck with Zeshan and Zeel in the first-year class. Shaking her head at the obvious ridiculousness of it all, Zeel turned to Madiha to see her sighing as well.

"Although I will never understand what you see in my toad of a brother, will you actually woman up and just tell him how you feel?" Zeel made Madiha snap out of her reverie with her direct question.

Still blushing, Madiha stuttered something unintelligible.

"What?" Zeel always enjoyed making her friend squirm this way. She knew very well about this gigantic crush Madiha had had on Zeshan since they were little kids.

"I said, you know it's not that easy, Zee! I'm not exactly in his league now, am I?", Said Madiha wistfully.

"His league? Maddy, my brother has like two brain cells. I'm pretty sure he lost one amid all the flashing cameras today. Trust me when I say this…he isn't out of your league. You are out of his league. And I think you better make it known to him. I'm tired of seeing you sigh this way as he flirts shamelessly with half the female populace of this college. In fact, while you're at it, just cut his ego down to size too. Maybe then he will actually fit into the t-shirt that just looks obscenely tight on him right now…"

"It's the muscles, Zee! Zeshan has the sexiest abs in this entire college…that t-shirt just clings to him in all the right places…" Madiha continued dreamily.

"Eww. Please stop talking. I'm going to gag." The pure look of disgust on Zeel's face made Madiha burst out laughing. However, before she could respond to her friend, their attention was drawn toward the front of the room where Principal Chitre had just entered with a very flustered-looking Vice Principal Jaywant Tawde hot on her heels.

"Silence!" One booming word from the principal was enough to get everyone to stop talking.

Eyeing the mostly quiet room, she continued, "Good morning students! And welcome to St. Vincent's! While I know some of you have been a part of St. Vincent's Junior College, I am happy to see all the new faces who have chosen to join us this year. At St. Vincent's, education transcends the mere acquisition of knowledge and skills; it is an integral part of preparing each individual for their journey in life. The lessons imparted within the classroom walls hold incredible value, benefiting you immensely in the years to come, whether you choose to pursue higher education or venture into the professional world."

"Yeah right!" came a caustic remark from one of the benches at the back. Zeel turned around to see who had made the comment but was only met with a sea of blank faces. Why did there always have to be some smartass who thought it was cool to disrupt classes?

Unfazed by heckling, Principal Chitre continued, "To support your academic success, we have an outstanding faculty and staff who are dedicated to providing you with the best education possible. They will work with you to help you reach your full potential and achieve your goals. I also encourage you to take advantage of the resources available, such as our extensive library, state-of-the-art technology centre, and excellent extra-curricular programs. I expect each one of you to sign up for at least one of the many interesting clubs we have to help enrich your time here at St. Vincent's. We are cognizant of the pressures young people face today and; hence, we have an excellent mental health counselling program should you feel the need to speak with someone. For us, your emotional and mental well-being is as important as your academic success."

"Bullshit!" There he was again and this time he had even managed to garner a few supportive sniggers from some of the other students. Zeel was irritated to find her brother among the ones supporting the mischief maker. She turned around once again but couldn't place the guy to whom the voice belonged. Rolling her eyes in irritation, she turned her attention back to the woman at the front of the class.

Unperturbed by the obvious insult, Principal Chitre went on about the agenda for the meeting, "Before you all disperse to your academic wings to begin classes, I wanted to lay down a few rules and make some announcements."

There was an audible groan from the backbencher, followed by a very loud "Fuck the Rules!" now drawing several hoots and whoops from those in agreement. This time when Zeel turned around, she found a face staring straight at her. He had hazel eyes that were currently boring into her, challenging her to stand up and report him. His was a handsome face, with unruly black hair falling in careless abandon across his forehead, giving him the appearance of just having rolled out of bed. Even though she desperately wanted to, Zeel couldn't take her eyes off him. That was all the invitation he needed to give her a taunting smirk which finally made her snap her gaze off him, anger rolling off her shoulders in quiet waves. He knew he had rattled her. The snort of derision she heard from behind her confirmed as much.

Zeel turned her attention to Principal Chitre who looked like she clearly had reached the end of her patience. Pushing her spectacles up her nasal bridge, the woman looked straight at the boy with hazel eyes and said, "I know for you college is nothing but a momentary interlude in your long career as a professional degenerate, however, there are others here who would actually like to study and earn a degree. So, could you please reserve your remarks for the end of my address, Mr. Chitre?"

***

Chapter 2

St. Vincent's College was one of the premiere higher education institutions in Mumbai city. Located next to a rocky beach the college was a popular choice for most because of its academic excellence. More importantly, the college had the best program for Psychology in the country. The only reason why Zeel had even decided to apply to the college in the first place.

Ever since she was a child, Zeel had been fascinated by human behaviour and had wanted to become a psychologist. Many would have thought that the whole scandal with her sister Zinia in St. Vincent Jr. College would deter Zeel from applying to the Arts program at St. Vincent, but they were wrong. Nothing could stop Zeel from going after her dreams.

Having Zeshan in the same college wasn't her first choice, but at least they weren't taking the same classes. Zeshan was enrolled in Mass Media and spent most of his day in the media wing with his buddy Raunak, who was also in Mass Media. On the flip side, Madiha, being a real math whiz, opted for the Science program. Zeel felt a bit sad about not having her trusted friend around, but she was thrilled for Madiha. She not only got into the cool Science program but was also trying for an International Mathematics Scholarship that could lead to studying in Switzerland.

Despite all the excitement about Madiha's achievements, Zeel didn't feel too great walking into her Sociology class, one of the compulsory foundation courses she had to take in her first year of college. She truly wanted to enjoy her first year of college. Only, her idea of enjoyment included working really hard and studying even harder. The little scene at orientation had left her irritated.

At orientation, she had been shocked to find out that the heckler and the 'professional degenerate' Principal Chitre was referring to was none other than her son Advait. Never in a million years could have Zeel imagined that the stern looking Manjiri Chitre, with her Ph.D. in Economic Analysis and Policy, the same Manjiri Chitre who had also been an advisor to some top politicians and had worked closely with key government bodies, who was the Principal of a premier educational institution in India had spawned a creature like Advait Chitre! The stark contrast between them was almost comical.

Right as she entered the classroom, there, before her stood Advait, embodying every horrible quality that was in total contrast to her perfectly organized life. He was the ultimate rebel, shaking up her carefully crafted world. His outfit? Totally against the norm, with ripped jeans and a black t-shirt with some satanic-looking band logo that stood miles apart from her neat and tidy style. His arms were covered in tattoos, with one even peeking out from under the neckline of his t-shirt. And his hair? Like he has just tolled out of bed but still somehow managed to look incredibly good.

Wait, what? Good? No. The hair did not look good. It was messy and unkempt. Zeel quietly chastised herself for having weird thoughts. This boy really had done a number on her brain. There was definitely nothing good about him. His mother was right, professional degenerate seemed like a title that was made for him.

Despite all of this, it was his sheer audacity that really got under Zeel's skin the most. Right there in the classroom, as he casually puffed on a cigarette, a bold defiance gleamed in his eyes, as if he were challenging her directly. He dared her to step up, his mischievous grin silently beckoning for a response. It was like an open invitation to a showdown, a clash of stubbornness she hadn't asked for, but somehow found herself irresistibly pulled into.

Standing there, clutching the edges of her impeccably organized notebook, Zeel felt a surge of irritation mixed with an undeniable curiosity. She couldn't help but resent him for shattering her comfort zone, disrupting the tranquillity she was desperately trying to cling to at that very moment. However, beneath her annoyance, a tiny spark ignited—a spark she was certain had nothing to do with his intense gaze and everything to do with the anger welling up inside her.

Zeel had been annoyed all day, and it finally reached a breaking point. She decided to do something about it. Enough was enough. She stepped up to Advait, with a look of determination and extreme annoyance flashing across her face. She quickly took his cigarette away, showing she wouldn't put up with his rude behaviour. She crushed the cigarette with her ballet flat, ending the little showdown satisfyingly. If he knew how to break the rules, she knew how to handle those who broke them.

Zeel thought Advait would get mad and hit back, but she saw his eyes flash with anger as he got up, all tall and tough-looking. He seemed like he worked out a lot, and his strong arms hinted at playing some intense sport. This made her even more mad because he looked like an athlete but still chose to smoke.

She braced herself for a showdown when she looked back at him, ready for an argument or even a fight. But what she got was totally unexpected – he burst out laughing like he'd gone crazy. He just looked at her and laughed, making Zeel feel like she was losing her mind. This guy wasn't just a troublemaker; he was completely insane!

Caught off guard, Zeel now felt a sense of unease around this peculiar yet undeniably hot boy standing before her. Before she could react, Advait's laughter subsided, and he leaned down slightly to whisper in her ear, "You couldn't resist doing that, could you?"

The gravelly quality of his whisper, combined with the lingering scent of tobacco, sent a shiver down Zeel's spine. She turned to face him, only to find that infuriating smirk he had given her during orientation still plastered on his face.

Zeel cleared her throat, her voice laced with restrained annoyance. "Excuse me, but last time I checked, this wasn't the college's designated smoking area."

With a glint of amusement in his eyes, Advait took another leisurely drag from his cigarette. "Oh, I must have missed the sign," he drawled, his voice dripping with sarcasm.

Zeel's lips curved into a sardonic smile. "Well, consider this your friendly orientation. Smoking isn't just hazardous to your health; it's also hazardous to the patience of everyone forced to endure it."

A chuckle rumbled in Advait's throat, his eyes locking onto hers in a way that sent a ripple of something unfamiliar down Zeel's spine. "Ah, I see. So, you're the self-appointed crusader for everyone's comfort, is it?"

"I'm just the voice of reason, something you clearly seem to be lacking" Zeel retorted, a spark of determination flickering in her eyes. "Now that I've put out that cigarette, I'm going to go back to ignoring you. You've taken too much of my time anyway."

Advait raised an eyebrow, a spark of challenge in his gaze. "Well, well, Zeel Kapoor. Daughter of the silver screen power couple and a leader of the Shaming Smokers Squad? Who would've thought?"

Zeel's fingers tightened around her book; her retort poised on the tip of her tongue. She leaned forward, her glasses sliding slightly down her nose as she shot him a pointed look. "Who would've thought, indeed? But just remember, the only roles you play here are 'delinquent' and 'nuisance.' And trust me, those don't usually get sequels."

Advait's laughter echoed in the quiet classroom, a sound that was unexpectedly warm despite the edge in their exchange. He kicked the cigarette butt that Zeel had just crushed beneath her foot, his smirk now softened into something resembling genuine amusement.

"Well, Zeel, I'll keep that in mind as I contemplate my character development," he replied, a glimmer of something more thoughtful behind his eyes.

***

Anything related to society, culture, and social change had been a lifelong passion for Zeel. She had embraced this passion from a very young age, even as a precocious eight-year-old. Zeel took a courageous stand against her housing society's unjust treatment of maids and handymen, who were forced to use a separate elevator, so the more affluent and snobbish residents could avoid sharing space with them. While her older sister Zinia reluctantly supported her little sister, Zeeshan, engrossed in his video games, showed little concern for such matters. Surprisingly, their father stood by Zeel, leveraging his star power for the first time to instigate a positive change.

Zeel should have been thrilled to be in her Sociology class, especially with the class being taught by the renowned author and social activist, Savita Thakkar. However, she couldn't relax enough to focus on the lecture. Throughout the entire hour, Zeel sensed Advait's eyes intently following her every move, every breath.

Every so often, she could feel Advait smirking at her from the back of the class which was obviously ridiculous. Even so, she couldn't shake the feeling off and was clearly unable to focus on what Professor Thakkar was saying.

"Miss Kapoor, what do you think?"

On hearing her name, Zeel snapped out of her Advait-addled reverie and whipped her head up to see Professor Thakkar staring straight at her, clearly expecting her to say something.

"Ummm…" Well, shit. She had never been caught off guard in class like this. She was the annoying kid who always knew the answers to every question. She was the overzealous student who spent her summer vacations reading not only storybooks but also textbooks for the next school year. And here she was, that same studious Zeel, who, forget about knowing the answer, didn't even know what the question was.

"Professor, if I may?" Came a confident voice from behind her.

Professor Thakkar, who wasn't going to wait all day for Zeel to answer, nodded.

"Well, you know, it's a complex dance between society and individuals. Society can certainly shape us, just like some people who are shaped by their obsession with control and order. But, as we've seen, individuals can also shape society, like when someone decides to take it upon themselves to play the hero and stomp out other people's freedoms – like certain unwarranted acts of cigarette confiscation, for instance. It's all about finding the right balance, I guess," Zeel whipped around to face Advait, whose sly smile showed how much he was enjoying seeing her seethe with rage.

Zeel couldn't believe that not only had this annoying guy made her so conscious that she hadn't been paying attention in class, but now, he was also mocking her in front of the entire class! What made matters worse was that Professor Thakkar looked impressed with his answer.

"Very interesting Mr. Chitre. Considering your perspective on the interplay between society and individuals, can you share your thoughts on how something as seemingly trivial as a cigarette can be symbolic of personal freedom and a challenge to societal norms? Do you see this as a microcosm of larger social dynamics?"

Turning on the charm, a sly smile still in place, Advait answered, "Well, Professor, let's not forget that even small acts of rebellion, like say smoking a cigarette in class, can make quite a statement. It's like society saying, 'You can't smoke here,' and the rebel saying, 'Watch me.' So, to answer your question, perhaps for a smoker, a smoking habit is just his way of, you know, shaping society, one puff at a time. And I must say, it seems quite liberating. Don't you think?"

Professor Thakkar laughed. She actually laughed at Advait's ludicrous answer. How could an intelligent woman like her be charmed by a turd like Advait was beyond Zeel's comprehension. In that moment if Zeel could roll her eyes any harder, they would roll right off her face!

Not wanting that delinquent to have the last word, Zeel's brain had finally caught up with her tongue, "Well, Mr. Chitre, if your cigarette puffs are considered your grand contribution to society, I suppose we're headed towards a future where the progress of society is gauged by the number of ashtrays filled, rather than the minds ignited."

The sneer she wore while saying this could have easily sent any troublemaker packing, but Zeel couldn't tell if Advait had picked up on the disdain in her words. All she could see was a genuine smile on his face, one that lit his entire face, complete with a subtle hint of mischief dancing in his eyes, partly concealed by his strikingly long lashes. It unsettled her that he appeared genuinely intrigued by their verbal banter. Before the moment could stretch any further, the bell chimed, interrupting the class.

"Well, students, thank you for making this a very interesting class. I cannot wait to hear more of your views on this topic Mr. Chitre. You too Miss Kapoor. I foresee some interesting conversations emerging as we go along."

With that, Professor Thakkar wrapped up the class, assigning them some readings for the next class. Zeel was already itching to track down the texts the professor had listed and sink her teeth into them. But first, she had to get rid of the tall shadow hovering over her. She looked up from her seat to see Advait standing next to her desk.

"What do you want, Chitre?"

"From Mr. Chitre to Chitre in less than a minute, huh?"

"Is there a point to this conversation?"

Advait leaned casually against the desk, a glint of amusement still dancing in his eyes. "Oh, I just wanted to say that I appreciate a good challenge, Miss Zeel Kapoor. You certainly know how to keep a conversation interesting."

Zeel couldn't help but roll her eyes. "Don't mistake a verbal exchange for anything more, Chitre. I'm here to learn, not to entertain you."

Advait chuckled, seemingly undeterred by her dismissive tone. "Fair enough. But you might find that the best learning often comes from the most unexpected places. Anyway, I won't keep you from your studies. Enjoy your reading, Miss Kapoor."

With that, he pushed off from the desk and sauntered away, leaving Zeel both annoyed and, perhaps just a little intrigued. The encounter had left her with more questions than answers, and she couldn't help but wonder if there was more to Advait Chitre than met the eye.

***

Chapter 3

"Earth to Zeel!"

Why was Madiha staring at her funnily, Zeel wondered. "Huh?"

"Huh?! Who are you and what have you done with my friend Zeel Kapoor?"

"Stop being dramatic, Madiha."

"Dramatic? Zeel, you just added ketchup to your coffee. And I'm the one being dramatic? Right!"

Sure enough, there it was a gloopy blob of the red condiment in her latte. Horrified at what she had done, Zeel finally snapped out of whatever daze she was in and pushed away her coffee and also the plate of *pakodas* (fritters) which had long grown cold. She looked sheepishly at Madiha who looked very concerned.

"Babe, is everything okay? Are you unwell? Is it Zeshan? Did he do something to annoy you?"

"Madiha, why does everything have to be about Zeshan? Can you please just ask him out, go on a date with him, find out he sucks, dump his sorry ass and get over him already?"

"Whoa whoa whoa! Slow down, girl! Don't bite my head off. I was just worried about you okay? I've never seen you this way before. What's bothering you?"

Realizing she was being mean to her best friend, Zeel said, "I'm sorry Madz. I'm just really irritated. God! I hate that Chitre!"

"Principal Chitre? Why? What has she done?" Madiha, bless her heart, could be completely oblivious to the world at times.

"Not her, silly. Her son! Advaid Chitre. He's the worst!" Zeel stomped her foot under the table.

"Oooh are you talking about that absolute hottie from orientation?"

"He's not that hot." Zeel huffed.

"Oh, he totally is. And you know it." Madiha teased.

"Madiha, please! He smokes."

"So he's smokin' hot!" Madiha cackled at her own lame joke leaving Zeel to roll her eyes for the second time in the day.

Seeing Zeel about to lose it, Madiha tried to rein in her laughter, and said, "Okay okay! He's not that hot. He's just a little hot though."

"Madz!" Zeel flicked a balled-up tissue paper at her friend but finally joined in the laughter. It was hard to stay mad at Madz.

"So…it's this not-so-hot guy, that's got you daydreaming huh?" Madiha asked with a smirk.

"Which poor guy are you girls gossiping about?" asked Zeshan who had just walked into the cafeteria with his friend Raunak, who as always, just looked bored to be there.

"Umm…no one," said Madiha, turning slightly pink.

"Let me guess, he's fictional?" teased Zeshan.

Turning her annoyed gaze towards her twin, Zeel said, "Why don't you go entertain your groupies instead of annoying us?"

"At least my 'groupies' are real and not some dashing hero who only exists in some dirty romance novel!"

"Get lost Zishu!" Zeel chucked another balled-up tissue at her brother. At this rate, the college would have to start fining her for littering.

Zeshan ducked to avoid the incoming projectile which narrowly missed his shoulder but couldn't stop laughing at the look on his sister's face. Madiha seemed to be enjoying the banter amongst siblings too. The same couldn't be said about Raunak though who looked rather restless now.

Popping one of Zeel's *pakodas* in his mouth, Zeshan stuck his tongue out at her and started to walk away with Raunak in tow, but not before flashing a dazzling smile at Madiha which sent her heart into a tizzy.

Rolling her eyes at her brother's retreating figure, Zeel turned towards Madiha and continued with their ongoing conversation, "I wasn't daydreaming. I was just a little distracted. Mostly I've just been angry the whole day. First with Zeshan being all ridiculous with the paps and then this guy. College was supposed to be my time, you know? It was supposed to be my escape from all the mess at home. And now I just feel like I've landed in a bigger mess."

Madiha reached across the table to hold her bestie's hand. "I know babe. Don't worry. It's still your time. Don't let the boys rain on your parade. Okay? Why don't we chuck that yucky ketchup coffee and head to the library?"

Zeel gave her a small smile. She was truly grateful for a friend like Madiha who just got her and knew what to say to calm her down. If there was one thing that could instantly brighten Zeel's mood was books! Nothing made her heart happier than the sight of endless bookshelves filled with books - each one promising a new story, a new idea, a new world to escape into. When reality got too much to bear, Zeel would happily get lost in a sea of words. Because, you know, the world in her books? It always made sense, no matter what.

"You're right. I need a break. I've been in classes all morning. My next lecture isn't until later in the day. Let's go." With that, the girls gathered their stuff and made their way to the main college building which housed the library.

***

The library was located in one of the older college buildings and boasted an enviable collection of over 60,000 books. Its grand wooden doors, smooth under the touch of countless eager hands often creaking when opened. Inside, the air carried the faint scent of aged paper and wisdom. Tall, regal bookshelves, their mahogany frames polished by generations of curious minds, lined the walls. The soft glow of antique lamps bathed the space in a warm, inviting light, creating a cozy retreat for the inquisitive souls seeking refuge within the pages of books both old and new.

When Zeel had first toured the college during admissions, the library was one of the first places she visited. It had been love at first sight. There was something magical about the entire place. The library was two storeys tall. The lower storey held the reading area and was surrounded by windows and columns of bookshelves on three sides. The upper storey, which was more of a mezzanine floor, looked inwards and faced the lower storey. It was connected by two spiral staircases towards the end of the reading hall and housed reading nooks flanked by bookshelves. The reading nooks provided ample privacy if you wanted to escape the world for a little while…so that is exactly where Zeel was headed.

The girls picked out the books they needed for their respective papers and made their way to the mezzanine floor for a couple of hours of uninterrupted study. The first few reading nooks were occupied by other students. Not in the mood to share a table with the others, the girls decided to move in further. Towards the far end of the library, they finally came upon an empty table. It was only when Zeel went closer to the bookshelves, she realised why this little nook was empty - the shelves were filled with books on taxation. No one was going to bother them here!

Madiha had already set up her laptop and was ready to work on some Maths problems. Zeel had just started arranging the books she had pulled out for her sociology paper when she realised, she needed a paper punch for adding her notes to her binder. Most of the tables at the library often provided these basic tools that students would need but theirs didn't seem to have one.

"I'll just be back Madz," Zeel quickly decided to zip into the nook next door to grab the paper punch.

As she turned the corner past the bookshelf splitting the reading spots, she almost froze. Bad luck hit hard because right there he was, none other than Advait Chitre. But this time, he wasn't alone. A girl with long black hair and a seriously short skirt was all over him. Crazy enough, they were making out right there in the library!

For what seemed like forever, Zeel stood frozen, jaw dropped, eyes fixed on the unexpected spectacle. If the girl hadn't let out a quiet moan, Zeel might've stayed there for God knows how long looking utterly clueless. Snap out of it, she thought. Zeel chose to grab the paper punch, discreetly turn around, and leave, but a laid-back voice drawled from behind, "Stalking me, Miss Kapoor?" making her drop the paper punch with a clatter.

***

Chapter 4

Letting out a breath she didn't realise she was holding, Zeel slowly turned around to face her nemesis. In fact, the gorgeous girl who was sucking his face just minutes ago was also staring at her now, her eyes shining with anger. Advait, on the other hand, seemed to be enjoying seeing Zeel squirm.

Zeel's cheeks flushed with embarrassment, and her mind raced to find the right words. "Stalking? Yeah right! I have better things to do than follow you around," she retorted, trying to regain her composure.

Advait smirked, a mischievous glint in his eyes. "Really? Because it seems like you just couldn't get enough of me and had to interrupt a lovely moment, I was having with dear Saloni here." He gestured towards the girl, who shot Zeel a venomous glare.

Attempting to deflect the awkwardness, Zeel crossed her arms defiantly. "Well, it's not my fault you chose the library for your romantic escapades. Some people actually come here to study; you know."

Advait chuckled, unfazed by her sarcasm. "Who said we weren't studying, Miss Kapoor? Perhaps you're the one with the wrong idea." He winked at Saloni, who smirked in response.

Zeel felt a surge of frustration but decided not to engage further. "Whatever, Chitre. I have more important things to do than waste my time on you." With that, she turned on her heel, determined to leave the scene and the awkward confrontation behind.

As she walked away, Zeel could hear Advait's laughter echoing through the library. She couldn't shake off the feeling that he enjoyed getting under her skin. The encounter left her feeling a mix of annoyance and confusion. What was his game, and why did he seem to revel in making her uncomfortable?

Getting back to her seat empty-handed earned her a confused look from Madiha. Preferring not to say anything, Zeel just shook her head and decided to focus on the texts in front of her instead. For some reason, she couldn't stop thinking about Advait's hand on Saloni's waist and how he had held her so close to his chest.

Zeel was trying really hard to read the pages in front of her, but after reading the same paragraph five times without registering a word of it, she was almost about to give up. Just then, a movement caught the corner of her eye, and she looked up to see Advait standing in front of her.

"You dropped this when you ran," he said handing her the paper punch, his eyes daring her to deny it and plunge into a web of half-truths in front of Madiha.

"You can put it on the table and leave," said Zeel, curtly.

Advait chuckled, leaning casually against a nearby bookshelf. "Well, well, the prim and proper Miss Kapoor isn't just ignoring books today but also seems to have forgotten how to say, 'Thank you,'" he commented with a sly grin, deliberately needling her in a way that struck a nerve.

Zeel shot him a withering look, her patience wearing thin. "Thank you? You expect gratitude for returning something that you made me drop in the first place?" Her tone was sharp.

Advait raised an eyebrow, seemingly unfazed by her irritation. "I was merely trying to be a gentleman and helping you out. You can put those claws back in, Zeel." He pronounced her name with an emphasis that irked her further.

Rolling her eyes, Zeel snatched the paper punch from his hand. The brief touch of his fingers against hers sent little shockwaves across her skin, a sensation she deliberately chose to ignore. "Gentleman? Please, spare me your false chivalry. I'm perfectly capable of picking up my own things without your assistance."

Advait grinned, enjoying the banter. "Ah, but where's the fun in that? Besides, it's not every day I get to rescue a damsel in distress from her fallen stationery."

Zeel scoffed, her frustration reaching its peak. "I don't need rescuing, and I certainly don't need it from you. So, if you're done with your little act, I suggest you find someone else to bother."

Advait straightened up, his playful demeanour giving way to a more serious expression. "You know, Zeel, you're quite entertaining when you're all fired up. But let me make something clear. I'm not here to bother you. I just find you very intriguing."

"Intriguing?" Zeel repeated, incredulous. "Is that what you call it? Flirting with Saloni one moment, tormenting me the next? If this is your idea of intrigue, then I'd rather not be a part of it."

Advait's eyes glinted with mischief as he leaned back, a smirk playing on his lips. "Jealousy looks good on you, Zeel. Didn't think you had it in you."

Zeel scoffed, crossing her arms defensively. "Jealous? You've got to be kidding me. There's nothing to be jealous of. I am, however, questioning Saloni's taste in men."

Advait chuckled, his tone dripping with amusement. "Oh, come on, Zeel. Don't pretend. It's written all over your face. Saloni and I were just having a little fun, and you couldn't handle it."

Her cheeks flushed with a mixture of anger and embarrassment, Zeel shot back, "Fun? Is that what you call it? Your version of fun involves making others uncomfortable?"

He tilted his head, studying her with a playful glint in his eyes. "Well, technically, we were just making ourselves comfortable. You deciding to watch us while we made out, is on you. Not me. Also, it's not my fault if you can't handle a bit of competition. Saloni and I were just testing the waters. However you, I must say, seem to be swimming in the deep end, Zeel."

Zeel gritted her teeth, determined not to let his taunts get to her. "I'm not interested in your games, Chitre. I have more important things to focus on than deciphering your questionable intentions."

Advait chuckled again, his words laced with mockery. "Questionable intentions? Zeel, you underestimate me. I'm just trying to keep life interesting. Clearly, it's working, considering the shade of green you're turning."

Annoyance flashed in Zeel's eyes. "Save your games for someone who cares. I'm not playing along."

Advait winked, his teasing demeanour unfaltering. "You say that now, but deep down, you love the challenge, don't you?"

Before Zeel could respond, Madiha looked up from her laptop, curiosity etched across her face. "Is everything okay here?"

Zeel glanced at Madiha, then back at Advait. "Everything's fine. He's just leaving." She emphasized the words, gesturing toward the exit with a pointed look.

Advait chuckled, stepping back. "Until next time, Miss Kapoor. I know you'll step up to it," He said with a wink.

With that, Advait sauntered away, leaving Zeel seething with a mix of frustration and an unexpected twinge of uncertainty. The library suddenly felt too small, and the enigma of Advait Chitre lingered in the air, leaving Zeel with more questions than answers.

***

The rest of the day passed in a blur. Zeel was just about ready to run home the moment the last lecture for the day concluded. After the disastrous day she had had, all she wanted was to curl up in bed with a nice fantasy book.

She was just about to step into her house when her phone suddenly went off. She had learned to ignore the all-too-familiar chime of the social media app. It was probably some post about Zeshan. She had notifications for each of her family members set on her phone. Not by choice of course. It was Zeshan who had added them giving her yet another reason to be annoyed by her twin.

As she was about to unlock the front door and step inside, her phone went nuts again! It was like a bunch of messages crashing in all at once. In a rush, she flung open the door, tossed her bag on the floor, and swiped up to see what the commotion was all about. What popped up on her phone screen made her freeze in her tracks.

As Zeel opened each new notification, the colour slowly drained from her face, and her heart sank. No! This couldn't be happening. It just couldn't. With wide eyes, she frantically opened her messaging app, only to find countless messages and memes already circulating everywhere. And there, right on her phone screen, was her mother, captured on film, lips locked with some actor called Nihar who was half her age. To top it all off, her mother looked completely wasted in the video. The most horrific thing was that the actor seemed to have posted this video himself to gain clout.

With shaking hands, she dialled her mother's number, but it was switched off. Desperately wanting to call her sister Zinia, she was well aware that Zinia was in Paris dealing with her own scandal. Before she could dial Zeshan's number, her phone started ringing. It seemed that Zishu had also seen the video.

"Zee, where are you?"

"I just got home."

"Stay there. Raunak and I will be home soon."

"Where's mom Zishu?"

"Jigna's figuring that out. I'll call you."

"Zishu…" but he had already hung up.

The one thing Zeel craved more than anything in this world was not to be thrust under the spotlight. However, being part of a very famous, very dysfunctional family was not exactly the most conducive environment for her craving. Her mother had often been caught on camera drunk and causing a scene, but this time it was way worse.

Picking up her things from the floor she walked over to her bedroom dejectedly only to find her phone ringing once again. Thankfully, it was Madiha.

"Hey Zee, you okay?"

"No. Not really."

"I know babe. I know this sucks. I'm coming over."

"No. You don't have to do that."

"You don't have a choice in that matter Zee. I'm already on my way. I'll be there in five minutes. Whatever you do, just do not keep scrolling any further, okay? All these paparazzi social media handles are just disgusting."

"I know…but they're not reporting anything false, are they? It is clearly Mom in those videos. And she doesn't exactly have a spotless past."

"I know Zee. Still. It's just a whole lot of crap."

"I know."

"I'll be there in five, okay?"

"Okay."

Despite Madiha's explicit instructions, Zeel found herself opening the app to see what was being said about her mom. While she had expected the usual memes and sneers from trolls, what completely caught her off guard was a particular media outlet that had uploaded a video, asking her father's 20-something girlfriend, Kanika Singh about her boyfriend's ex-wife's shameful public display. Zeel could never stand that woman, and at that particular moment, she felt the urge to slap her. The anger rose within her as she heard the woman word-vomiting in the video.

"Oh, Adhira has always been like this. I mean, why do you think Raghav left her? How could he stick around with a woman who seems to have no clue about right and wrong? Three grown-up children and this is how she behaves? Disgusting, isn't it? It really makes you wonder about everything that went down with Zinia a couple of years ago. I mean, with a mother like that, what on earth will the poor children end up learning? My heart just goes out to Zeshan and Zeel. They're such good kids, you know..."

Zeel had just about had enough of Kanika's crap. It was rich of her to question Zeel's mother's character when she herself had slept with a married man - Zeel's father! To top it all off, Kanika was also a terrible actor; Zeel could see the fake concern dripping from her face right through the phone screen. Just as Zeel was about to scroll further, something in the video caught her attention, making her stop in her tracks. While dispensing her nonsensical opinions, Kanika was clutching her pearls, quite literally, and right there on her ring finger was the biggest diamond Zeel had ever seen.

For the second time in less than ten minutes, Zeel felt the ground beneath her feet shifting. The unsettling sensation, akin to the rug being pulled out from under her, left her momentarily off balance. It suddenly made sense why her mother was so drunk! That rock on Kanika's finger was all Zeel needed to see, a glaring symbol of a reality she had not fully grasped until now. Her father was engaged to his girlfriend and her mother was heartbroken all over again.

A searing pain stabbed deep within her, a cruel echo of the past when her father had walked out on them, witnessing her mother crumble. The thought of seeing her endure that heartache once more was unbearable. Inhaling a shaky breath, she mustered the courage to dial her dad's number, hoping against hope that he could somehow avert the impending storm and spare her mother from reliving the devastation all over again.

"Hello...Zeel?"

"How could you do this to her, Dad?"

"Zeel…"

"Let me guess. You didn't even inform her yourself, did you? You just let her find out on her own. Am I right?"

"Zeel, you need to understand, that there's no way to talk to your mom rationally."

"So, what did you do, Dad?"

Raghav Kapoor went eerily silent at that.

"Tell me now!"

"Zeel…I…well, we wanted to keep it under wraps. But Kanika and I, bumped into Adhira at an event earlier today and she saw the ring. She went completely crazy!"

"What so you expect? You'll are still married! Or have you forgotten that?" Zeel had gone almost silent. The pain too much to bear.

"Didn't your mom tell you?" Raghav sounded genuinely surprised.

"Tell me what?" Zeel asked in a whisper, "Tell me what, Dad?"

"I sent her divorce papers yesterday. I guess which is why she turned up at the event. She wasn't even invited you know…" His voice suddenly trailing off.

"Oh my god! Oh my god! Dad, when did you become so heartless? So cruel?" Zeel was sobbing once again.

"Zeel…I know I could have handled it better."

"Handled it better? Are you for real? I know you don't care about being married to mom anymore, but do you not care about your family either? Instead of behaving like a mature human being and discussing things, having a proper conversation, you just send papers? Just like that?" Zeel didn't stutter. Not once.

Raghav sounded downright ridiculous when he said, "This has nothing to do with you kids, Zeel."

"Nothing to do with us? Our parents are getting a divorce, our father is engaged to someone else, our mother is heartbroken and God knows where right now, and you're telling me it has nothing to do with us? You know what, I am ashamed to call you my father. You do not deserve a shred of love or respect from any of us."

"Zeel!" Raghav seemed to have found his voice all of a sudden, clearly angry at being called out by his own daughter.

"No, Dad! You don't get to 'Zeel' me! Look what you've done. Wasn't leaving her, leaving us, enough? Wasn't flaunting your girlfriend at every party, every social gathering enough? Why did you have to do this, Dad? Why do you hate her so much? Why do you hate us so much?"

"I don't hate you Zee…you know that! And what happened today, I am not the only one responsible for it. Your mother was completely aware of what she was doing when she was getting blackout drunk!"

"You are the reason she is an alcoholic! You can't just absolve yourself from all responsibility you know!"

"Zeel, you're too young and too angry right now to understand anything. I need to go. I cannot talk to you about this anymore."

And with that, he hung up.

There he was. The great Raghav Kapoor. Gaslighting his own daughter. Zeel let out a sob that seemed to come from somewhere deep within her. She was hurting. She was hurting for her mom. She was hurting for herself. She was hurting for the shitstorm her family would have to face all over again thanks to her father's thoughtless act.

***

Chapter 5

It had been three days since Zeel had attended college. Madiha had been kind enough to get her notes from all her classes, not that Zeel could focus on anything to get any studying done. She was definitely behind on all her assignments and papers. But she couldn't really bear to think about anything else but her mother who was currently holed up in her bedroom. She had been speaking with Zinia who had offered to come home right away but Zeel had asked her not to. Jigna, Zeshan's excellent publicist, had advised against it. There's no rest for the wicked and clearly nowhere to hide for those who live their lives under the spotlight.

It had been three days since Adhira had spoken a word. Jigna had been the one to locate Adhira. Of all the people, a paparazzo whom Adhira had been kind to during her heyday as an actress had let her hide it out in his car after she was spotted leaving the bar where the now-infamous kiss had been discreetly filmed. He was also the one who had called Jigna to collect Adhira. Ever since Jigna and Zeshan had brought Adhira home, all she had done was lock herself up in her room and cry.

It had been three days since Zeshan had gone and broken Nihar's nose, the young actor who had posted his mother's video online. The actor had threatened to press charges against Zeshan, but to Zeel's surprise, Raghav Kapoor had called the actor and assured him that he would end the guy's career if he even considered harming Zeshan in any way. Although this did not diminish Zeshan or Zeel's anger towards Raghav, it did spare them from dealing with another scandal, at least.

It had also been three days since Zeel had received an intriguing message on her phone which she had almost missed amid all the media queries and social media notifications - two words from an unknown number which read, "You okay?"

She had ignored the message earlier, but her curiosity had finally won, prompting her to respond with "Who is this?"

"You wound me Ms. Kapoor," came a response within seconds.

"Do I know you?" she asked.

"I should hope so. First you take away my cigarettes, then you question my date's taste in men and now you refuse to recognize me?" read her screen.

Zeel's eyes almost bugged out of her head the moment she realised who she was texting with. How had he gotten a hold of her number? "How did you get my number?"

"How about you answer my question first. Are you okay?" he continued to be annoying through texts as well.

Zeel had seen enough of the world to know that when a scandal broke, it often exposed two kinds of people: 1. Those who thought the worst of you and made it a point to steer clear of you, fearing that your misfortune might rub off on them. And 2. Those who wanted to know all the inside details so they could go and spill the tea in the media to further their own selfish needs.

She was trying to work out what Advait's angle was. He obviously wasn't steering clear of her. But neither did he seem to be the kind of guy who would spread rumours or gossip. He seemed to be the kind of person who often marched to his own drumbeat. So why was he messaging her?

Out of curiosity, Zeel asked, "Why do you care Chitre? Aren't you happy I'm not in college to stop you from doing whatever illegal, immoral, unethical activity you're obviously indulging in?"

That got her a smiling-face-with-sunglasses emoji followed by enough hahahas bring a tiny little smile to Zeel's face. This guy was obviously crazy.

"Where's the fun in doing something like that when there's no one to catch me breaking the rules, Ms. Kapoor?" he responded with a smirking emoji at the end of his message.

To that, Zeel responded with her own rolling-eyes-emoji. She knew how this game was played.

But then, his next message kind of surprised her, "Listen, are you really okay?"

She stared at the message for a really long time before responding with, "I'm okay."

"Good. I'll see you in college."

That was all. No messages after that. This little message exchange had left her with so many questions…some she didnt even know if she wanted the answers to.

***

Zeel couldn't stay at home forever. The next day, gathering all her courage, she decided to go to college. Zeshan wasn't exactly keen on facing the media, who were definitely camped outside their college. Mainly because he wasn't sure if he could control his temper if any of them asked some stupid questions about his mom. As luck would have it, Madiha wasn't going to be in college today either. Her class was attending some math symposium on the other side of town. So, it was going to have to face the music all by herself.

The night before, Jigna had come over to coach her, to make sure she knew how to handle the media. It wasn't her favourite thing to do, being told how she should speak and behave in public, but she got it. Avoiding the media was not going to be an option. So, there she was, practicing the canned responses Jigna had printed out for her while she was on her way to college.

As expected, the media that usually just about tolerated Zeel, if not completely ignored her, pounced on her like hungry hyenas waiting for their first meal of the day.

"Zeel! Zeel!"

"Zeshan nahi aaya?! (*Zeshan didn't come?*)"

"Adhira ma'am kaha hain? Phirse boyfriend ke saath. (*How's Adhira ma'am. Is she with her boyfriend again?*)"

She knew it was going to bad. She did not realise she would have this intense urge to punch the guy who had asked her this. Schooling her emotions, Zeel adjusted her glasses and started walking faster, only to be intercepted by some more photographers keen on snapping her pictures.

"Zeel, aapke papa doosri shaadi kar rahe hain. Aapko kaise lag raha hai? (*Zeel, your father is getting married again. How do you feel about it?*)" Screeched a young girl thrusting a mic in front of her face.

How did Zeel feel about it? Truth be told, she had been so busy trying to get her mom to stop crying and eat something over the last three days that she really hadn't had the time to think about anything else. Both she and Zeshan had been tiptoeing around the house, hiding TV remotes and phones from their mom so she didn't read some of the vitriolic stuff the media was reporting. Adhira was so wrapped up in her melancholy that she had even failed to notice the cut on Zeshan's lips, the one he had sustained when he had gotten into a fight with that jerk of an actor.

So, she wasn't lying when all she could mutter was "No comment."

However, it was clearly not the answer the hungry vultures were looking for. "Kucch toh bolo Zeel. Kya aapki maa bhi ab doosri shaadi karengi? *(Tell us something Zeel. Is your mother also going to get married again?)*"

Zeel tried to walk away from it, only to realise she was surrounded by media on all sides.

Yet another mike - this one attached to a phone which seemed to be livestreaming her misery - was thrust in her face. The human attached to it, asked, "Zeel, is Nihar the same actor your sister Zinia had also had an affair with? Are mother and daughter sharing men now? Will you also be dating him?"

Where did these clowns come up with shit like this? "I need to go. I have class." Zeel could feel her heartbeat rising. As hard as she tied to push through the throng of reporters and photographers, it just felt like they weren't going to let her go unless they got some reaction out of her. One of them even tried to grab her hand in a bid to stop her from walking away.

Snatching her hand away Zeel finally screamed, "Let go of me! How dare you touch me! I told you all, I have no comments for you. Let me go to class."

However, nothing could deter the horde. "Zeel! We heard Nihar has moved in with you mother. Both of them haven't been spotted since the video came out. What can you tell us?"

"Nothing. She's already told you she has no comments for you. So stop hounding her!" came a booming voice from behind Zeel making her jump. Turning around, she saw none other than Advait standing behind her, with a menacing scowl etched across his face, casting an ominous shadow over the unfolding chaos. Quickly glancing down at her, she could see the softening of his eyes and a quick quirk of the eyebrows, as if to ask her if she was okay. She nodded without thinking, dazed by what was happening around her.

"Who are you to tell us to get lost?" demanded one of the media persons.

Completely ignoring the journalists, Advait grabbed Zeel's hand, "Let's go?"

Nodding, she started walking after him. She was acutely aware of her sweaty palms and the slight tremor in her hands as she took his. While she had tried to put up a brave face in front of the media, she was a nervous wreck on the inside. And then to be rescued by none other than the one guy who had been the antithesis of everything she held dear just made her realise how cruel fate really was.

"Yeh kaun hai Zeel? (*Who is this Zeel?*)"

"Tera boyfriend hai kya? (*Is he your boyfriend?*)"

"I thought she was also dating Nihar."

"Aren't you going to kiss him Zeel? We could do with one more juicy video!"

Advait stopped so suddenly that Zeel almost crashed into him. Turning around, he took one look at the sleazy gossip rag 'reporter' and walked up straight to him, flexing his shoulders. Suddenly, a hush fell over the entire group. "Advait, please, let's go," Zeel found herself pleading from behind, almost certain that Advait was going to break the guy's jaw.

Coming to halt in front of the reporter, Advait grabbed the guy's collar and said loudly for everyone to hear, "Tereko kiss karu? Aur bhi accha video banega. Phir daalna apni site pe, acche views milenge. (*Why don't I kiss you? It will make for a better video. You can put it on your site then, you'll get good views for it too.*)"

The ridiculousness of Advait's response had managed to shock everyone around for a moment, including Zeel. Turning around, Advait grabbed her hand once again, "Let's go. This circus ends here."

By the time the media had recovered from what had just happened, Zeel and Advait were safely inside the college gates, away from the journalists, half of whom were laughing at what Advait had done, while the other half trying their best to find out who this guy was.

This entire time, Zeel's heart had been beating like crazy. Finally, she could feel her pulse slowing down. Nothing made sense. How could the media be so insensitive? How could people ask such things? Was there nothing called privacy? What was this obscene curiosity that people had for knowing every dirty detail of celebrities' lives? And what the hell was wrong with Advait Chitre? Of all the things that had happened, Advait's presence was the thing that had rattled her the most.

Looking around her, of course she had expected people to stare at her, what with her mother's scandal and all. But what she couldn't figure out was why did they all look surprised? It was only when she they had reached inside the corridor to the Arts wing of the college did Zeel realise that she had been walking inside the college premises while still holding Advait's hand.

Hastily snatching her hand out of Advait's Zeel uttered something that sat between a 'sorry' and a 'thank you'. What was wrong with her! She could feel her cheeks heating up. Advait, curse him, was laughing at her.

"Thanks for…" she started but then stopping, not knowing how to end the sentence.

Advait smiled at her, the smile lighting up his chocolate brown eyes, "See you later, Ms. Kapoor."

"You didn't need to…" again, she didn't know what to say.

"If he asks, give him my number, okay?" said Advait suddenly.

"I'm sorry?" Zeel was totally confused.

"The reporter. He really seemed to be into me," Advait made a face of mock lust and let out an unholy laugh, slowly backing away from Zeel, giving her a quick wave.

In what felt like a million years, Zeel found herself smiling. As annoying as Advait could be, in that moment, Zeel had a lot to thank him for.

As he walked away from her, Zeel finally took her phone out of her bag and saved the number she had been texting with all this time under the name 'Professional Degenerate.' The smile that Advait had put on her lips lingered there for the rest of the day.

***

Chapter 6

By the time Zeel was done with her last class, her phone was blowing up with messages yet again. And there were about ten missed calls from Zeeshan, and some from Jigna. She had somehow managed to go through the day and had avoided responding to everyone - from inquisitive classmates to overly sympathetic professors. She had also managed to evade the few photographers that were camped outside the college before slipping into the cab. So, the barrage of messages on her phone could only mean that something else had gone down while she was busy with her lectures.

Letting out a deep sigh, Zeel called Zeeshan back. The moment her phone connected, his angry retort made her stop short, "What is wrong with you, Zeel? Isn't what we're dealing with already enough for you? Did you have to go and add to the whole media circus?"

Zeel couldn't understand why Zeeshan was losing it. She hadn't said a word to the media.

"What are you talking about Zishu? I haven't said anything to anyone!"

"I don't think you understand, Zee. You not saying something could also lead to a media scandal for us," he responded.

Zeel was totally confused, "What do you mean?"

"What happened at college today?" Zeeshan asked.

"Nothing. I reached college, the media was there, I didn't say anything and then I went to class." answered Zeel.

"And?" prodded Zeshan.

"And, nothing."

"And what about Principal Chitre's son?" came the pointed question.

"Oh my god, Zishu, he just shooed the media off. Nothing else." She added, trying to sound nonchalant, but feeling far from it.

"No, Zeel. He did not just shoo the media off. He came to your rescue. And then he held your hand, and looked at you like you were the only person in this world that mattered! And then he picked a fight with a journalist - for you. So now you tell me, what the hell were you thinking?" When he put it that way, Zeel could see how this entire thing could look really bad.

"Zishu, you don't know what it was like. The media were just pouncing on me! He was just trying to help…"

Zeshan cut her off, with an angry, "Well he didn't. Why don't you go online and check what stories the media is writing about you? We'll talk then!"

He hung up without warning.

Zeel was also on the verge of losing her patience. More than anything, today she was struggling to understand how Zeshan was even related to her, let alone being her twin. Zeshan knew her well. He knew how she avoided any kind of attention. And Advait wouldn't have to step in if Zeshan would have been there in college by her side. But he chose to take the easy way out and avoid the media altogether. So, he had no right to lecture Zeel now.

Reluctantly, Zeel opened the social media app to see what lies were being spewed about her. She didn't have to scroll too long. Within moments of logging on, she was greeted with pictures of her and Advait looking into each other's eyes - the silent moment between the two where he was checking on her twisted into something ugly by calling it something it wasn't - a look of lust. There was another account which focused on their intertwined hands and how Advait had gallantly stepped into rescue his girlfriend. Some accounts had even gone far enough to create montages of the two of them with a filter of pink hearts set to popular Bollywood love songs.

This was bad. So much for wanting to stay out of the spotlight. Zeel would have laughed at the irony of it all if she wasn't the one at the receiving end. After what had just gone down with her mom, the last thing Zeel wanted was yet another news cycle with a Kapoor caught in the headlines. But that's exactly where she was now, wasn't she. Life was just throwing her one curve ball after another.

She picked up her phone and dialled Zeshan, "Tell me what to do now?"

"You do nothing. Come home. I've called Jigna over. We need to discuss a strategy to navigate this mess."

***

"How well do you know this boy?" Jigna was busy typing out a message to someone on her phone while simultaneously interrogating Zeel.

"I don't. I just met him on the first day of college." Zeel was trying hard to concentrate on her coffee instead of trying to worry about Jigna's scary questions.

"So, he asked you out on the first day?" Jigna was still typing that message.

"No, he didn't. I scolded him for smoking in college."

"He smokes. Hmmm. What else do you know about him?" That was one long message.

"Nothing really. Just that he's the principal's son. And she thinks he's good for nothing. He likes to argue with everyone. Gets into trouble often. Oh, and I caught him making out with some girl." That made Jigna's head snap up in attention.

"What girl? Do you know her? Is she, his girlfriend? How did you find out?" Jigna almost tripped over her own tongue in the hurry to get these questions out.

"Saloni. Nothing. I don't think so. And they were making out in the library."

"Why don't you think she's his girlfriend?" Asked Jigna, her eyes narrowing suddenly, as if she was trying to focus on the answer in Zeel's mind.

"Because he said so. He was just having some fun. He doesn't come across as the serious types. I mean, his own mother calls him names. Also, he's kind of full of himself. I don't think he even thinks or cares about anything or anyone else."

"But he cares about you." Jigna's statement made Zeel suddenly look up at her in surprise.

"What do you mean?"

"Zeel, that boy jumped into the media fray to help you out. And from what I can see so far, he hasn't made any kind of a media statement to get any attention. He hasn't even responded to the ridiculous claims some media people are making that he said he wanted to kiss one of those male reporters present there…" Zeel's sudden giggle made both Jigna and Zeshan, who had been sitting next to Jigna and scowling the whole time, stop and stare at her.

"Oh my god, he actually said that. To Ramesh Ji from Bollywood Tamasha? Are you serious?" Jigna suddenly looked like those cartoon characters whose eyes roll out of their sockets when they're surprised.

Zeel nodded trying to control the giggles that had suddenly engulfed her, almost choking her on her coffee.

Zeshan looked like he was looking for a nice hard spot on the wall to bang his head against. Because according to him, the women in his family were clearly out of their minds. Jigna, who was largely passive and monotonous with her questions so far, suddenly became a lot more interested. Putting her phone aside, she got up from her seat, and suddenly exclaimed, "I think I know what we can do."

"What?" Zeshan was the first to ask.

"I think we could use this," she continued.

"Use what?" Zeel asked.

"This little incident that happened today. We could actually use this to our advantage." Jigna had that look about her - the too-happy-to-be-thinking-about-doing-nothing-good - look. There was definitely some evil plan brewing in that brain of hers.

"How do you think we can do that?" asked Zeshan.

"Simple, get Zeel and Advait to confirm their relationship."

Zeel spat out the coffee she was drinking with a start. "Are you out of your mind?"

"What the hell, Jigna!" even Zeshan seemed annoyed.

"Guys, listen to me…" Jigna started.

"No Jigna, you listen to me. There is no 'relationship'," the angry quotes Zeel made with her fingers could have poked Jigna's eyes out. "I barely know the guy. And more importantly, I can hardly stand him most of the time. Yes, he did help me out in this one situation, but see where it has landed us. And you want me to take this further! What is wrong with you?"

"Exactly! I am not going to let my sister date some good for nothing loser!" came a totally unnecessary protest from Zeshan which only managed to further fuel Zeel's anger.

"Excuse me! What do you mean you won't 'let' me date someone?" There were those finger quotes again. "You may be my brother, but you have no right to tell me who I can or cannot date!"

"So, are you saying you want to date that guy?" Asked Zeshan.

"That's not what I am saying! Oh my god. It's like the entire world is hell bent on twisting everything out of shape!" Zeel got up from her seat in a huff intent on leaving the room.

"Hang on Zeel! And Zeshan, cut it out. Both you, just hear me out please!" Jigna implored the siblings.

"What?!" The twins yelled in unison.

"I am not asking you to date him for real! I want you to date him for the media. Right now, we need to get the media to shift their focus from your mother. From what I've found out so far, your father plans to marry Kanika before the end of the year, that means your mother will be under a lot of scrutiny and we have all seen how well Adhira handles all this. However, instead of letting the media focus on Adhira's outbursts, we could actually use this to our advantage and get them to focus on something positive, such as a budding new love…" Jigna tried to explain.

"There is no love," Zeel stamped her foot.

"Jigna, this is ridiculous," Zeshan chimed in.

"It may sound ridiculous, but just think about it. This is the kind of stuff media laps up and how. We can curate the entire romance to ensure the media writes exactly what we want them to write. And it helps keep the scanner off your mom," Jigna said.

"Even if we were to do this, and I am not saying we should… but even if we were to do this, you think this could look authentic enough?" Zeshan asked.

Zeel was surprised at how quickly Zeshan seemed to be coming around to the idea if he was already considering the option.

"I don't think that's going to be a problem," said Jigna, winking. "From the way that boy was looking at Zeel, I think he's already smitten. The romance will look real enough to the media. We will make sure it does."

That earned Jigna the dirtiest look Zeel could muster.

"Why are we even discussing this, guys? This is not happening. So could we give it a rest, please?" said Zeel in a determined voice.

"I mean, I know it sounds ridiculous, but Zee, Jigna has a point. I am not keen on seeing you date that jerk, but it does make sense. I have to agree with Jigna, it makes sense," Zeshan's argument made Zeel realise she was all alone in this.

"A moment ago, you were willing to wage a war for my honour and now you're ready to sell me out! Thanks brother!" said Zeel, her lip quivering with anger.

"Stop being so dramatic Zee. You know very well what I mean. All I care about is that mom is out of the news cycle. Don't you want that? Think about her!" If anything could soften Zeel's resolve, it was this. And Zeshan knew exactly how to press her buttons.

"Zishu, is there no other way?" Zeel pleaded.

"Okay, let's do this. Why don't you both think it over tonight? We can then decide tomorrow. Sleep over it." offered Jigna.

Zeel could hardly argue with that but she could still make her displeasure known. She stormed out of the room, her frustration and anger palpable. Zeshan, torn between family loyalty and the desire to shield their mother from the media storm, exchanged a conflicted glance with Jigna. The air in the room hung heavy with unresolved tension.

Jigna sighed, recognizing the difficulty of the situation. "Let her cool off," she suggested. "We'll reconvene tomorrow and discuss it with clearer minds."

As the door closed behind Zeel, the weight of the decision ahead settled on Zeshan's shoulders. Deep down, she knew the proposed plan, as ridiculous as it was, would throw the media off her mother's scent. But that did not mean she had to like it. For now, she was content in knowing that she had let her thoughts about this whole hairbrained idea apparent. Would she win this battle though, she had her doubts.

***

Turns out, all the fretting Zeel had done overnight had turned out to be completely useless. She had forgotten, when a crisis hits, all you can do is manage it and hope for the best. You do not have a choice in the matter. For when she woke up, there was yet another social media storm awaiting her.

Her mother had managed to get her hands on a phone, despite their best efforts to hide them all, and posted on her social media. It was a long, rambling post filled with rage she felt towards Raghav and his fiancé, Kanika. Reading each word was like a stab to the heart.

Zeel knew Ahira was hurting but couldn't really understand the pain. Seeing her parents' marriage fall apart had made Zeel wary of relationships in general. She couldn't understand how a well-read, well-educated, independent, modern woman would fall to pieces over a man this way. It had only strengthened Zeel's resolve to never fall in love.

This is exactly why she never allowed herself to have any crushes. She didn't fancy any boys in her school, never allowed herself to feel anything beyond mild appreciation for the work actors did in movies, she could also never understand Madiha's obsession with all those Korean popstars she kept fawning over all day. Zeel found solace in her books - both her study books, and her fantasy books. Sure, the fantasy books she liked to read featured romances, and it was okay to indulge in those, because her rational self knew the difference between fact and fiction. That was only fantasizing she was willing to indulge in.

So now, as she walked out into the living room to find Zeshan and Jigna already holding court there, Zeel already knew what she had to do. "So, how do we go about this?" she asked in a resigned tone.

***

Chapter 7

St. Vincent's had always been a childhood dream for Zeel. Yet, as she strolled toward the college gates today, a sense of dread settled in the pit of her stomach. Jigna had meticulously detailed the plan for an entire hour, but nothing about it resonated with Zeel. Despite the discomfort gnawing at her insides and the surplus of black coffees she consumed to quell the unease, she found herself stepping into the college, determined to see the plan through.

She thought if she could treat this like an academic project, perhaps it would help make sense of things. To maintain a systematic approach, she decided to document the plan's progress in a journal app on her phone—her way of ensuring she followed the playbook to the letter.

As usual, the media was camped right there. However, this time she had Zeshan by her side. "Ready, Zee?"

"Ready as I can ever be," she responded without looking at him.

The twins walked towards the waiting media storm. Within moments they were engulfed by the paparazzi, countless cameras and mics shoved in their faces, and questions pouring in from every side. Zeshan handled most of the questions, except one: *"Tumhara boyfriend kaha hai Zeel? (Where is your boyfriend?)"*

Taking a deep breath, Zeel responded, "He's not my boyfriend. And until yesterday I didn't even think he was my friend. But perhaps, I was wrong. So Advait, if you're watching this, I know we got off on the wrong foot earlier, but I'd like a do-over. Would you like to be my friend?"

While rehearsing the script earlier in the car, every word had tasted like a lie on her tongue. But now, as she addressed the media throng, she realised that she was actually mildly curious about what it would like to be Advait's friend. The boy was an enigma, filled with contradictions which simultaneously attracted and repulsed her in equal measure. But she couldn't deny that he intrigued her. Maybe, just maybe she could make this whole charade work. Hoping for the best, Zeel gave her best fake smile to the media and walked inside the college gates, leaving Zeshan to handle the rest of the questions.

***

"I leave you alone for just one day! ONE DAY! And you manage to land yourself a boyfriend? What the hell, Zee?" Madiha's anger was palpable as she confronted Zeel upon her entrance to the library later that day.

Before Zeel could offer any explanation, Madiha continued, "And you don't take my calls! You ignore my messages! What's going on?"

"Nothing is going on, Madz, and he is not my boyfriend. You should know that better than anyone!" Zeel finally responded.

"What's all this I'm reading in the news, then? Plus, everyone in college is buzzing about you and Advait being an item!"

"You know how the media likes to twist things, Madz," Zeel sighed.

"So, he never kissed you in front of the media?" Madiha asked, her eyes wide as saucers.

"He what? No! God! He just grabbed my hand to pull me away from the media. Jeez. Is that what they're reporting?"

"Yup! Now you see why I was upset. I mean, I'm your best friend. I call dibs on all the juicy details about your love life, not some Bollywood Mirchi Masala website," Madiha huffed.

Madiha's adorable outburst brought a smile to Zeel's face. "I know, Madz. You'll always be the first one I turn to. But as it stands, I do not have a life, let alone a love life. So, you don't have anything to worry about."

"Good. I'm glad. Anyway, what's the plan? I'm assuming you guys have already consulted Jigna on how to handle this?" Madiha asked as she arranged her books for their study session.

When Jigna explained the plan earlier that morning, this part made Zeel uneasy. To make the plan work and make her relationship with Advait look real, she had to keep the fact that it was all a setup secret from everyone except Jigna and Zeshan. Not even Madiha could know that Zeel was just pretending to be Advait's girlfriend, and this included Advait himself. Essentially, Zeel had to lie. And that was the one thing she hated above anything else in the world.

Suppressing her unease, Zeel forced a fake smile and responded to Madiha's questions, saying, "Yes. Jigna suggested I clarify with the media that Advait isn't my boyfriend. She also wanted me to offer him a hand of friendship."

Technically, Zeel hadn't lied, but she hadn't spilled the full plan either.

"Oh, interesting! So, are you going to talk to him in class and ask to be his friend, or..." Madiha inquired with anticipation.

"Um, well, I, uh, already asked him this morning to be my friend," Zeel admitted sheepishly.

"When did you manage that? Last I heard, he missed his morning classes because he was partying late last night," Madiha revealed.

"Wait, how do you know he was partying last night?" Zeel asked, curiosity lacing her words.

"I asked around... I was ready to go kick his ass for forcibly kissing you," Madiha confessed in a hushed voice.

"What? Why would you think he kissed me forcibly?"

"Well, there was no way you were going to kiss him willingly... so I assumed, you know!"

Zeel couldn't fathom what she had done to deserve such a supportive friend. Madiha truly was the kind of friend every girl needed. The fact that Zeel had to lie to her friend made the situation even more uncomfortable.

Zeel rose from her seat, enveloping her best friend in the tightest hug, exclaiming, "You're crazy. I love you!"

"I love you too, Zee! I know all this is really crappy, but I'm here to help. So just talk to me, okay?"

"Okay," Zeel replied, wiping at her suddenly moist eyes.

"Which brings me back to my question, when did you talk to Advait?" Madiha inquired, not one to let things slide easily.

Feeling cornered, Zeel finally admitted, "Well, I made a statement to the media. I asked him to be my friend in front of all the media people. If you open your app now, there will probably be a video of me saying as much."

Madiha wasn't easily surprised, but this revelation left her jaw slackened, and her expression said it all.

"Okay. Wow. Are you sure you're alright Zee? You, the girl who actively avoids being in the spotlight, you made a declaration in front of the media?" Madiha had an incredulous expression on her face.

"Well, Jigna said it would be best. You know, to further help establish the fact that Advait and I were'nt together," Zeel tried to explain hastily.

"Got it. I think. And I'm guessing he hasn't responded yet?" asked Madiha.

Zeel shook her head. She wasn't really sure if she even wanted him to respond.

***

Despite being the guy who always seemed to appear when she least desired it, Advait was surprisingly nowhere to be found. She hadn't heard from him at all since extending an offer of friendship two days ago. The media had been closely following the lack of progress, and according to Jigna, there was even a bet among the media folks on whether Advait would respond to her request or not.

Zeel had given up all hope of Advait ever accepting her friendship. Pitiful glances from people around her had already started, and she felt disheartened about putting herself out there. Jigna, for some reason, remained optimistic, which only irritated Zeel further. However, refusing to give up without a fight, Zeel decided to message Advait one last time.

"I know you've been busy partying and all, but it would be nice to get a response to my message."

Zeel had half-expected not to receive a response, but then she saw the three tiny dots dancing on her screen, indicating that he had received her message and was indeed responding.

"What message?" came the response.

When was this guy ever going to stop messing with her? "You know what message. The entire country knows it. The Bollywood press has made sure of that."

"I'm sorry I don't read trash." Coming from Advait, Zeel actually believed it.

"Oh, is it? Not as interesting as the porno magazines I'm sure you love to read?" Zeel thought to herself. Before she could type another word, came Advait's message, "It's cute you think I consume porn in print."

WHAT? Oh no! Zeel hadn't just thought it but had actually typed out the message about the porno magazines! To her chagrin, he continued, "Although vintage porn was really something, you know. There was a certain charm to it. That can't be said about today's porn culture, which is all about instant gratification."

What was even going on! Zeel was turning beet red reading the messages Advait was sending her. "Could you please stop talking about porn?"

"Well, you started it!" He was right, wasn't he? She had started it.

"I'm sorry, okay! I hadn't meant to send it," she responded sheepishly.

In response, she got a laughing emoji with an "I know. But it was fun teasing you. And also, if you want to know, I do read magazines. My favourite is the World Literary Review. I think you might enjoy it too."

Of all the things he could have said, she had not expected that. She religiously read the World Literary Review. She loved their monthly reading lists and book reviews. She responded to him, "I didn't expect you to be into literary reviews. You don't seem the type."

"And what type would that be? Smoking, skirt-chasing, partying, bad-boy?" He was mocking her now.

"Your words, not mine. But in a nutshell, something like that," Zeel admitted truthfully.

"That's okay. I'll let it slide. After all, you don't know me, do you? Now, only if we were friends, this would have been different," he responded, adding a winking emoji.

That rascal! He knew exactly what she was talking about when she had texted him, but he had to keep toying with her. "I can't believe I actually thought you hadn't seen the news about me asking you to become my friend. Thanks for making me look like a fool." Zeel just couldn't with this guy. How could he make her feel all sorry for judging him one minute and then mess with her the very next?

"You're many things, Zeel, but not a fool. Never a fool. And even you know that. Also, I was telling you the truth when I said I didn't read trash. My friends, however, is a different story. I was made aware of a certain pretty young girl asking for my hand in friendship. Must say, I hadn't expected that from you!" he said.

"Did you think you have a monopoly over surprising people? I can do that too. After all, you don't know me, do you?" Zeel knew how the game was played.

"Touche!" came the response.

"Now that I know you were made aware of my message, why haven't you responded to it yet?" she asked.

"That's not how friendship works, Zeel. You don't send a message through some reporters. What were you expecting me to do? Call a press conference?" he asked matter-of-factly. "Besides, I was busy."

"Busy doing what?" Zeel's curiosity took over.

"Busy helping a friend." he said.

"Saloni?" she asked. Zeel had no idea why she had asked that.

"What if it was Saloni?" came his response. She could feel him quirking his eyebrow in amusement. Why had she go ahead and ask something so stupid! What did she care who he was helping out? What was wrong with her!

"Nothing. You're free to do what you like. Help whomever you want to help," her attempt to cover up her gaffe felt lame even to her.

"Since you asked, no. It wasn't Saloni. It was a buddy of mine who needed some help. I wasn't in town," he said.

"Okay," she said.

"Okay!" He responded.

"So, will I be seeing you in college tomorrow?" she asked finally.

"I guess I'll have to accept your friendship in front of the cameras now, won't I? Kids these days…pics or it didn't happen… and all that!" he said.

His message made her lips quirk up in a small smile. He knew how to make her laugh, that was for sure. Maybe, just maybe this entire thing wouldn't be so bad after all. Zeel opened her journal app to tick the first leg of the plan off her list.

***

Chapter 8

Why Zeel expected Advait to act like a human being remained a mystery, even to her. True to his promise, Advait showed up to college, but he wasn't alone. Behind him stood an entire brass band, belting out all the popular Bollywood songs about friendship. And to top it off, he was energetically dancing to those very tunes. Advait had successfully captured the attention of the media, who were enthusiastically documenting his every move, along with a massive crowd of onlookers eager to understand the cause of the commotion.

If there was ever a moment when Zeel wished the earth would open up and swallow her whole, this would definitely be it.

"You have to hand it to him. The guy sure knows how to make a scene," said Madiha. Zeel had completely forgotten she had travelled to college with Madiha who was standing right next to her with her jaw somewhere on the floor.

When Advait spotted the three of them, he came dancing towards Zeel. And to her further mortification, got down on one knee and said, "*Kya tum meri dost banogi, Zeel Kapoor?* (Will you be my friend, Zeel Kapoor?)"

Kill me now! That was the only thought Zeel had as she saw Advait down on one knee. Fully aware of the cameras trained on her, she had no choice but to plaster a big fake smile on her face and say, "Yes!"

The moment she accepted his friendship, the media erupted into applause, providing Advait with an opportunity to get up and pull her into a bear hug. It happened so quickly that Zeel was taken aback. It was entirely normal for friends to hug, so why was she feeling differently? It wasn't unpleasant; in fact, it felt right. Which was weird. Zeel hadn't realised, underneath all the band t-shirts that Advait wore, were rock hard abs and a warmth that seemed to radiate through her. And it definitely didn't help that Advait smelled really good, like the ocean breeze with a hint of citrusy freshness. Zeel could imagine lingering like that with him.

Wait... that's not... that's not what she wanted. This was ridiculous. She realized she was still locked in that hug with him, "What are you doing?" asked Zeel through clenched teeth, ensuring her fake smile was still in place.

"You wanted me to make a public statement of accepting your friendship, didn't you? So here it is. Your public statement." he said as he pulled away from her and gave her a small wink.

"That's not what I wanted!" Zeel tried to protest.

But he stopped her with a "Didn't you?" before turning to the media waiting for their pound of flesh.

Just as he was about to begin answering media questions, a couple of security guards interrupted the little gathering with *"Aye, hato idharse!* (Move away from here.)*"* And right behind them, stood Principal Chitre with a murderous glare on her face.

***

"What is this behaviour? Such disruption is strictly in violation of the college rules! "Principal Chitre was on fire, and in the line of fire were Zeel and Advait. This is the second time Zeel was at the receiving end of Principal Chitre's anger, and once again, for no fault of hers. Principal Chitre had dragged them both to her office threatening severe disciplinary action against them.

"Mr. Chitre, for the last time, this is an educational institution. Not your personal playground. What were you thinking getting a brass band to play in front of the college?" clearly no one could ever accuse Principal Chitre of playing favourites.

"Exactly, it was in front of the college. Not inside the college premises. You don't have any say in what happens outside the college gates, so I don't know why you're getting so worked up over it," drawled Advait, who was currently leaning against the wall with a bored expression on his face.

In contrast, Zeel stood with her head bowed in shame, her fingers tightly gripping the back of the chair positioned in front of Principal Chitre's desk. Zeel was anyway awkward around any kind of authority figure. But to be in one's bad books? There was nothing worse for Zeel!

Principal Manjiri Chitre possessed a strict yet striking face. One could often see her wearing silk sarees, favouring cool colours, and she always wore her hair in a neat bun. Her glasses, whether perched on the bridge of her nose or atop her head, exuded simplicity and elegance. However, what truly distinguished her amidst her stern demeanour was her fondness for silver jewellery. Principal Manjiri Chitre seemed to possess an endless collection of silver trinkets, and presently, she was wearing a rather captivating tribal necklace. However, in that very moment, the jewellery she was wearing made Principal Chitre look even more formidable, which further added to the fear Zeel was already feeling. Zeel visibly shuddered at the look she was currently levelling at her son.

Realising there was no point in talking to Advait, his mother turned towards Zeel and said with the same severity, "Ms. Kapoor, I had expected you to be smarter than to encourage all this…"

"I'm sorry…" came a meek response from Zeel before Principal Chitre could even complete her sentence.

"Why are you apologising? You did nothing wrong," Advait interjected.

"So why don't you tell me whose fault it was, Mr. Chitre?" asked the principal.

"You know what, fine. Since you're so hell being on trying to make an example of all of this, go ahead and punish me. I don't really care anyway. I hate this place and you already know that, so whatever you say or do, doesn't matter to me," Advait said with his arms firmly crossed over his chest, with a petulant expression creeping over his face, "Let me guess, you want to suspend me? Go ahead. At least then I won't have to pretend to come to college every day."

"Suspension! Principal Chitre, surely it wasn't such a big offence. Please don't suspend him. He got the brass band to play because I asked for it," pleaded Zeel, knowing fully well that she hadn't asked for it. But she felt like the principal was being a bit too harsh. She wouldn't have done the same if it hadn't been any other student in the same situation. Also, as silly as it was, even Zeel agreed, what Advait did wasn't against the college rules.

Principal Chitre made a point to ignore Zeel and spoke directly to Advait, saying, "Suspend you? Why would I do that? Oh no. I have a better punishment in mind for you. For both of you. Not only do I want hundred per cent attendance from both of you, I also want you both to assist the librarian in cataloguing the books that were recently donated to the college by the renowned industrialist Mr. Sabuwala who also happens to be an alumni of St. Vincent's."

Upon witnessing Advait's initial objections, Principal Chitra raised her hand to silence him and proceeded, "Your classes conclude around 1 PM. I expect you to be present in the library every day by 2 PM, working until 6 PM for as long as necessary to assist the librarian in completing the required tasks. I won't entertain any objections from either of you. Mr. Chitre, since you requested a punishment, it's time to be responsible and accept it like an adult."

This time it wasn't Advait who objected but Zeel who said, "But Principal Chitre, we have assignments and papers we have to work on. This leaves us with no time."

"Considering your close friendship, why not collaborate on your assignments? I understand you have many shared classes. I can coordinate with your teachers to assign you as partners for joint assignments. As for your individual papers, the consequences should have been considered before the media attention you both garnered out there." said Principal Chitre.

"Absolutely not! I don't want to work on assignments with him! He hardly pays any attention in class. Most of the time, he's just arguing with the professors. I don't want to be the one completing all the assignments by myself while he contributes nothing!" Zeel responded anxiously, reverting to her previous demeanour before this entire charade unfolded.

"Hah! So much for wanting to be my friend. Thanks Zeel!" Advait shot her a dark look.

"Advait, one has nothing to do with the other. I care about my grades and my education. I can't mess with that this way." said Zeel.

"While I commend your dedication to your education, Ms. Kapoor, this arrangement is non-negotiable. Consider it a valuable lesson in collaborating with individuals you may not necessarily see eye to eye with. And Mr. Chitre, kindly temper the snark. Your indifference towards your future doesn't negate the significance others place on theirs. Now, if this matter is settled, you may both leave. I've already invested enough time in this issue," and with that, Principal Chitre concluded the meeting, dismissing them both.

***

Advait was the first to leave. Zeel had never seen him irritated, but her outburst had clearly touched a nerve. A part of her was irritated with him for putting her in this situation, while another part of her — the one that was already a big ball of confusion where Advait was concerned — was feeling guilty for exposing him this way in front of his mother. But what could she do? All the mess with her parents and now this added drama with Advait were seriously messing with her studies.

Madiha, like the good friend that she was, was waiting patiently outside the principal's office for Zeel. When she saw Advait brush past her with a dark look on his face, she knew something wasn't quite right.

"Zee, all okay?" she asked.

"Yes. And no."

Zeel saw the look of concern on Madiha's face and quickly filled her in on what had transpired within the office.

"Wow, no wonder he walked away angrily!" said Madiha, letting out a sigh.

"What do you mean? I don't even know why he was angry. I mean I know I said all that in front of his mom, but it's not like she didn't already know it," Zeel tried to reason.

"You really don't get it, Zeel?"

"What?" Asked a clueless Zeel.

"Zeel, based on what you've shared about the guy, one thing is clear. He's incredibly intelligent. Even if he's someone who doesn't care about authority, you've mentioned how his arguments in class, though frustrating to you, are not necessarily wrong; he presents excellent points. Passing judgment on someone like that seems unfair. Besides, we all know how demanding Principal Chitre is on him. I'm certain he didn't just get into this college because he is her son. She likely ensured he genuinely qualified, perhaps even making it more challenging for him. So, don't you think it's unfair for you to have said those things about him in there?" asked Madiha.

Realizing her mistake, Zeel understood that the whole act of wanting to be friends while also looking out for herself had unintentionally hurt Advait. This entire situation was going to be more challenging than she had anticipated when reluctantly agreeing to Jigna's plan. Releasing a breath, she didn't realize she was holding, she decided to head to class. Making things right with Advait was now a priority, but figuring out how to do that was a whole different matter.

***

Chapter 9

Despite Principal Chitre's express warning, Advait was not in class. In fact, he decided to bunk all the classes for the day. Zeel wasn't sure how she was going to make it up to him if she wasn't even going to be able to talk to him. She had debated sending him messages over the phone but gave up on that idea deeming it too impersonal especially after what had happened. It didn't help that the media, on the other hand was abuzz with pictures and videos of Advait going down on one knee and dancing for Zeel.

She had, in fact, even gone looking for Advait but gave up on her search when she realised, she was getting late to report to the library.

Lost in her thoughts, Zeel entered the library later that day for her meeting with Mr. Anupam Sawant, the librarian, regarding the punishment. She was surprised when she saw Advait already there, engrossed in conversation with him.

"I'm glad you could join us today, Ms. Kapoor," said the librarian.

"I'm sorry for being late," she said. Advait didn't even bother to look at her.

She sighed inwardly. This was going to be a lot harder than she had anticipated.

For the next hour or so, the librarian explained what needed to be done. The task was simple enough. Both of them would have to work together to create a proper digital catalogue of each of the books from the donation pile, they would then have to label them accordingly and stack them in the right places. Principal Chitre would have had to hire interns to do this job, but clearly, she was killing two birds with one stone her.

Having grasped the assignment, the librarian led them to the back room, which would serve as their makeshift 'office' for the foreseeable future. The room was simple, featuring a small window, a slightly shaky ceiling fan, a couple of chairs, and a table with an old computer and printer—all neatly arranged against one wall. While the decor left much to be desired, what greeted Zeel against the opposite wall significantly dampened her spirits. Anticipating around a hundred books to be catalogued, she soon realized, from the massive crates pushed against the back wall, that she might be spending the entire semester confined to this cramped space!

"You've got to be kidding me Anupam! It's impossible to get through all these books even in three months!" Advait's statement mirrored Zeel's thoughts. She was also a little surprised at how causally he had called the librarian by his first name. The man was at east fifty years old.

"Come on son! I know this isn't difficult for you. In fact, I daresay you'll even enjoy the process. From what I know about Mr. Sabuwala's collection, you're likely to find some real treasures in these chests!" said the librarian.

"I'm not debating that, Anupam. But this is a lot to get through," said Advait.

"Well, in that case, you should be thankful that you have someone to help you here, don't you?" said Anupam glancing over at Zeel.

Advait chose not to acknowledge what Anumpam had just said, which further grated on Zeel's nerves.

"So, anyway, I've got to attend to some other important matters. I'll leave you kids to sort this out then. If you need anything, feel free to ask me. I'll be in my office. There's already a task sheet I've created and shared with the two of you; send me an update at the end of each day so we can track the progress. Any more questions?" Anupam said, clearly ready to move on.

"No more questions," replied Zeel. "And thank you for this."

With that, Anupam gave one last encouraging look to the two of them before leaving them to the task at hand.

"So, what do you want to begin with first?" asked Zeel. She doubted Advait could ice her out forever; he had to talk to her at some point, or this task would take an entire year to complete.

Without saying another word, Advait got to work, opening the crates and stacking books on the table, leaving Zeel to figure out the digital cataloguing using the painfully slow and old computer.

So that's how it was going to be: pin-drop silence punctuated by the occasional grunt and the whirring of the computer fan.

After nearly two hours of working in silence, Zeel finally asked, "Do you want to take a break? I can handle getting the books out while you make the entries."

"No thanks. I want to make sure my contribution to this assignment is evident," came a snarky response.

"Advait, I'm sorry, okay? I was really stressed out. With everything that's happening, I didn't want yet another thing to go wrong," Zeel tried to reason with him.

"I don't need your apologies, Zeel. You make a whole song and dance about how the media misrepresents stuff when they write about you or your family. But what do you do? You make assumptions based on a few stupid encounters and paint me to be someone who is unreliable and incompetent. And this is something you've been doing since day one with me. What have I done to you, Zeel, that you seem to hate me so much?" The intensity in Advait's eyes made Zeel's cheeks redden.

"I don't hate you," said Zeel in a small voice.

"I know you didn't really want to be friends with me. That was probably a stunt your publicist put you up to, but you went along with it. Hell, even I went along with it. But if you can't even be civil, this isn't going to work," he said. He was absolutely right, wasn't he. But the problem wasn't that Zeel didn't want to be civil to him. The problem was something else entirely.

"It's not that I don't want to be friends with you. It's just you confuse me, okay!" said Zeel, finally admitting out loud what she had been feeling all this time.

"Confuse you?" That seemed to have caught his attention, for suddenly, Advait looked very intrigued. He took a step closer to Zeel, looked straight into her eyes and asked, "What do you mean?"

"I mean you're obviously smart, but you don't apply yourself at all…and still all the teachers seem to like you. You clearly have some bone to pick with your mother, I mean Principal Chitre, but you're actually really nice to all the other professors. You don't care about the rules at all, but mostly you just seem to do it for fun and not because you want to actually cause trouble. And for the most part, I feel like you just want to irritate me and trouble me, and then you go ahead and do things for me which just confuse me!" Zeel blurted out.

"What confuses you about it, Zeel?" Advait had moved in even closer.

Zeel was acutely aware of his presence; she could feel her pulse racing as his hazel eyes met hers. His gaze seemed to challenge her to reveal more of herself, something she had carefully hidden from everyone else. "What confuses you, Zeel?" he asked again.

Without intending to, Zeel blurted out, "How one moment you could be making out with Saloni in the library, and the very next, telling me that you find me intriguing. How you challenge me all the time in class, and yet when I was surrounded by those vultures, you swooped in to rescue me. How you don't even talk to me properly but were the only one to message me asking if I was okay. Mostly, I think I don't like you, but then..." That's when she ran out of things to say because, just like Advait had moved closer to her, Zeel realized she had also been moving closer to him, close enough to touch him.

"But then what, Zeel?" Advait's voice came out in a whisper, his eyes intent on finding the answer in hers.

Zeel hesitated, feeling a mix of nerves and excitement. "But every time I'm with you, everything just feels different. I can't explain it. There's this weird connection, and when you're not around, it's like I'm always looking for you. It confuses me."

She looked away, embarrassed by her honesty, but Advait gently pulled her back, his hand on her chin, ensuring she met his gaze. "You confuse me too, Zeel. But I'm not avoiding it. I want to dive into this confusion and learn more about you. From the moment I first saw you, I felt drawn to you. I'm willing to explore what's between us, but we need to be on the same page for it to work. I want to understand what we feel when we're together," Advait admitted.

Encouraged, Zeel continued, "It's like there's this magnetic pull, and I can't resist it. Logic escapes me when I'm near you. When you're not around, I find myself searching for something only you seem to fulfil. It's confusing, but it's also..."

Before she could finish, Advait gently placed a finger on her lips, silencing her. "Don't overthink it, Zeel," he whispered. "Feelings don't always fit neatly into words. It's okay to be confused."

Understanding the rush of emotions, Zeel moved closer to his touch, her gaze fixed on his. In that wordless connection, Advait gently cupped Zeel's face with one hand, his other hand finding her waist, drawing her nearer. Zeel's heart pounded against her chest, but she eagerly embraced the fading distance between them. Her eyes conveyed her eagerness and that was all the signal Advait needed. He leaned in gently and brought his lips crashing onto hers. Their lips met, the kiss soft and hesitant at first, but with each passing moment, growing stronger as they both poured their unsaid emotions and desires into it. Their bodies entwined together mirrored the rhythm of their wild lips.

As they pulled away, both were left breathless, their eyes locking in surprise and also, understanding. The library, witness to the evolution of their relationship, held the secret of this unexpected turn. Uncertain of what lay ahead, Zeel and Advait stood in the hushed atmosphere, aware that this kiss had altered the course of their connection, opening a new chapter filled with promise and uncertainty.

***

Chapter 10

It wasn't supposed to be like this. This was not a part of the plan. Developing actual feelings for Advait was never a part of any plan. And yet there she was, Zeel Kapoor, finding herself inexplicably drawn to that frustrating boy with hazel eyes and tattoos all over his arms, who challenged her at every step and drove her totally up the wall. At the same time, he was also the same guy who made her feel things she had never felt before, who made her feel safe and cared for, who made her feel seen for who she was rather than for which family she belonged to.

It had been few hours since that life-altering kiss, Zeel's first ever kiss. There was something innately special about being able to share it with Advait who didn't just excite her physically, but also engaged her mentally. Zeel had expected to feel awkward after the first kiss, but somehow things just felt easy with Advait. She still had a million questions and a ton of confusion to wade through, but she decided to take Advait's advice and jumped headlong into it, which is why she had spent the entire evening glued to her phone, asking him all kinds of questions.

"You have siblings, right?" She started with the easier ones.

"Yes," he said, "Two. My brother who is currently trying to break into the Indian cricket team, Atharva. He's good but can be even better. And my little sister, Anuya. She studies in our college too. But she's in the 11th grade."

Zeel vaguely remembered Zeshan mentioning something about it on their first day of college.

"And are you close to them?"

"To Anuya, yes. She's my little baby. Atharva, not so much. He's a good guy but can be too intense for my liking. My mom loooooooves him. So, you know what it's like."

Zeel chuckled at that and then she softly broached the topic, "What's the deal with you and your mom? Why the animosity?"

"Want to know all my deep dark secrets on Day 1, is it Ms. Kapoor? Let me maintain this mystery a bit longer," he said teasingly.

"Deep dark secrets? Do you have many of those?" Zeel asked.

"You never know. But am I an open book? Probably not. There are parts of my life that I don't really talk about to people. Most people don't care, and the others would love to use your weakness to their advantage.," he said like the wise 18-year-old guy that he was.

"Very deep and very true. Look at me, anything and everything I do, becomes a headline," said Zeel ruefully.

"I hope I'm more than just a headline to you, Zeel," said Advait.

Advait's sincere question left Zeel feeling a bit uneasy, especially considering she had already marked 'kiss' off her journal app earlier in the evening. However, she did it more out of her obsessive-compulsive need to stay organized and follow the rules than as a way of tracking her progress in setting up a fake relationship with Advait.

"I don't care about headlines, Advait. At least not the ones that feature me. And you should know that too. However, I hope I'm more than just one of your conquests," said Zeel.

"My conquests!" Advait let out a booming laugh at that.

"What?" Asked Zeel.

"Who do you think I am, Zeel? Some modern day Cassanova who's out there seducing every woman with a pulse?" he asked, still laughing.

"Well, I wasn't the one making out with…who was that… ah…Saloni, a few days ago," taunted Zeel.

"Wow! You really are jealous, aren't you?" teased Advait.

"I'm not. I'm just stating a fact. Oh my god, now that we're discussing it, please tell me she isn't your girlfriend and I am not being an idiot," Zeel was suddenly panicking on the inside.

"What makes you think she could be my girlfriend?" Advait was clearly enjoying toying with her.

"Well, she was all over you and you seemed to be enjoying it," said Zeel.

"Did you actually see us making out?" asked Advait.

"I was right there, Advait. Remember?" she said.

"Yes, but did you actually see us kissing?" he asked again.

Now that she thought about it, she hadn't actually seen them making out. She had seen him holding her really close. But no, she hadn't actually seen them kissing.

"Umm…no," she offered tentatively.

"Exactly. And that's because we weren't kissing." offered Advait.

"What do you mean?" Zeel was confused once more.

"Saloni is a good friend of mine. She just wanted to make her ex-boyfriend jealous. So that's what we were doing. Pretending. Not making out. I don't have a girlfriend, if that's what you want to know. In fact, I've never had a serious girlfriend." admitted Advait.

Zeel didn't expect this kind of honest disclosure from Advait. But then again, he had never lied to her about anything, so she had no reason to not believe him about this.

"What about you?" he asked her, "Any guys waiting in the wings to destroy me because I dared to touch you?"

"Besides my brother, no one." said Zeel, with a smile in her voice.

"No psycho ex?" he prodded.

"I've never had a boyfriend," she admitted.

"Not even a fling?" he asked.

"Nope," she said.

"Wow," Advait took a long pause before asking, "Zeel, was this your first kiss?"

The question genuinely made Zeel blush. She mumbled a quiet yes into the phone.

For a moment she thought she had lost the connection, because she was met with total silence on the other end of the line. "Advait, are you there?"

"Yes. I'm here." he said.

"I thought you hung up. I mean I know I'm probably not a good kisser. It's ok. I...I...," Zeel just realised she had unlocked a new fear.

"Zeel. You were perfect. You are perfect," said Advait. "Now, all I have to do is, make sure to kiss you every single day."

If Zeel wasn't blushing earlier, this statement definitely turned her beet red!

"Stop it!" said Zeel. "I have to go. Zishu is home. I need to speak with him."

"Only on one condition," said Advait.

"What?"

"Kiss me."

Zeshan entered the room just as Zeel was kissing the phone. She was mortified at being found out by her brother and hastily hung up. She could still hear Advait's laughter at the other end. That boy was going to be the death of her!

***

The next morning, Zeel had woken up with a smile on her face. Talking to Advait had been a refreshing experience. Dare she say it was better than reading her favourite fantasy books. However, she knew this feeling wasn't going to last long because later in the day she had a meeting with Jigna who wanted to know what had transpired in the principal's office. Zeel had avoided talking to Zeshan about the whole thing the night before, claiming to be really tired. But she knew she wasn't really off the hook yet. She would have to offer them something, if not the whole truth.

"Jigna's on her way," said Zeshan who was already at the breakfast table, scrolling through his phone.

He seemed content enough with the way the whole piece with Advait's declaration of friendship had gone the day earlier. Their mom was out of the news cycle and reining the airwaves was his sister Zeel and her new 'friend' Advait. As far as Zeshan was concerned, it was now time for the next step in the plan.

Zeel grabbed an apple before flipping open her own laptop to read some more stupid headlines. She realised the entertainment media really had nothing better to write about than make up stories and analysing ridiculous little nothings. Apparently, a news channel had even run a panel discussion about whether a boy and girl can indeed be friends or not. Zeel couldn't believe she was witnessing this in the 2020s. For a moment she truly thought she had time travelled to the 80s.

It wasn't long before Jigna turned up for her quick regrouping with the twins. She was intent on knowing every little detail of Zeel's interaction with the principal and was actually pleased to learn about the punishment.

"Ah! That is wonderful news. You can now actually use this time to get closer to him," she said.

Zeel kept her head down and made a non-committal little sound.

Zeshan didn't seem too pleased. "I don't like the idea of you being locked up in some dingy room with that guy for hours every day. It makes me extremely uncomfortable."

"Zishu, please. It's not like he's going to do anything to me," Zeel said trying to hide the blush which was definitely creeping up on her face.

"Zee, he's a guy. If I was locked up in a room with a pretty girl, there's no way I wouldn't be trying my luck with her," Zeshan said making a face.

"Well, he didn't try his luck. He barely even spoke to me," said Zeel.

"He hasn't yet. But I'm sure he will. He seems the weaselly type," venom dripped from every syllable Zeshan uttered.

Rolling her eyes, Zeel said, "Isn't that what you guys wanted? For me to enter into a relationship with him? Then why are you so worried about what he will say and do. Don't you want him to hit on me."

Zeshan was clearly having second thoughts, for he said, "I know I agreed to go ahead with this plan, but at any moment, if you feel even the tiniest bit of discomfort, we're calling it off. We'll deal with whatever shit is flung at us in the media."

Zeel couldn't fault her brother for trying to look out for her. As misplaced as his concern was, she found it sweet. "Thanks Zishu. I'll keep that in mind. Now, if I'm not needed anymore, I'm headed to college. Madiha is waiting for me outside."

With that, and a quick peck on Zeshan's cheek, Zeel rushed out of the house, eager to get away from her brother and the publicist.

***

"How was it?" asked Madiha, the moment Zeel opened the door to get into the car.

"How was what?" asked Zeel, who was fully aware of what Madiha was referring to.

"Zee! Tell me! How was it working with him yesterday? Was he pissed? Was he okay? Did he say anything? What happened?" Madiha clearly wasn't going to give up until she got all the details.

However, just before Zeel could respond to her incessant queries, her phone went off. She made the mistake of checking it in front of Madiha because Advait had not only wished her 'Good Morning' but also sent her a kiss emoji.

"Woah, wait a minute! What's that?" Madiha exclaimed, pointing at Zeel's phone. "I'm not prying or anything, but why did that look like a message from you-know-who?"

Zeel had been caught. Being new to the whole dating thing, she didn't even know how to hide it. In fact she wasn't even sure if she and Advait were dating. They'd shared a kiss and talked all night, but that wasn't exactly dating was it?

"Hello! Don't spaz out on me girl! Spill the beans now! What is going on?" Madiha asked, her penguin earrings bouncing with her curls.

"Um…nothing, just Advait wishing me good morning. Yesterday was good. I apologised and we worked things out," said Zeel, trying to hide as much as possible, but failing miserably because there came a few more pings on her phone, each lighting her screen with a new kiss emoji.

"Right…and now he's sending you virtual kisses? What am I missing Zee? What are you not telling me?" Insisted Madiha.

"Nothing to tell, Madz," Zeel tried to play it cool, but unable to contain it any longer, she finally blurted out, "Just, you know… we kissed."

Zeel immediately hid her face behind her palms.

"OH. MY. GOD." Madiha screamed so loudly, the driver thought she was being assaulted or something.

"Madz!" Zeel tried to get her friend to keep calm.

"ZEE! WHAT. THE. HELL?" Madiha was clearly never going to get over it.

"Madz, please stop. I'm already blushing okay!" said Zeel.

Within moments, Madiha embraced her best friend and then eagerly prodded Zeel to spill every detail in the most excruciating manner. The girls spent their commute dissecting every word Advait had uttered and analysing his reactions. By the end of it, Madiha was thoroughly convinced she had a front-row seat to the best new rom-com in town. However, Zeel's stomach was in knots because, despite everything, she felt like she was keeping way too many secrets from everyone she loved, and sooner or later, it was all going to come back to haunt her.

***

Chapter 11

"Hey, what are you doing this weekend?" Zeel was busy cataloguing a set of books on India's political history when Advait popped the question. It was Friday and both of them were keen to finish the work for the day before heading home.

"Working on my assignment," said Zeel, her eyes still trained on the screen in front of her.

"And when you're done working on it?" he asked again.

Finally turning her attention away from the screen, Zeel looked at him and said, "What do you have in mind, Mr. Chitre?"

"I wanted to take you somewhere," he said.

"Where?" she asked, curiously.

"Somewhere," came the cryptic reply.

"I'll need a little more than that," Zeel insisted.

"Okay, I kind of wanted to introduce you to some friends of mine. That is, if you're up for it," he said.

That was not what Zeel was expecting to hear. They hadn't explicitly decided to hide their relationship from anyone but since neither of them were keen on all the media scrutiny, they often kept their distance from each other during class, only choosing to get together when working in the back room of the library. So, when he brought up the idea of meeting his friends, the first thought Zeel had was that of instant panic.

"Advait…I would love to, but with the media and all…I don't know," said Zeel.

Not only was she worried about the fact that the moment the media got wind of them hanging out together, Jigna would insist on making a whole song and dance about it, but also that she wasn't really ready to share Advait with the world yet. She had enjoyed these past few days of getting to know him at her own pace.

While she knew that Advait was into music, and also played the drums very well, there were still a lot of things about him that were completely new to her. For instance, she was absolutely shocked to find that Advait was a state topper in the board exams and had in fact been accepted into three engineering colleges. She was equally shocked to find out that he had represented India in several chess tournaments when he was in school. She would never have him pegged as a nerd, but essentially, that's what he was. And the knowledge made her immensely happy. She felt a whole new level of connection with him.

She was lost in her thoughts when he said, "Where I'm taking you, the media won't be there."

That sounded weirdly ominous. She asked hesitatingly, "Umm, where exactly are you taking me?"

"I want to keep that as a surprise," he said. "So, would you still like to join me?"

Common sense was at odds with curiosity in her mind. Curiosity finally won over and she said, "Fine. Tell me, where should I meet you?"

Advait told her to meet him at a metro station on the absolute other end of the city, a place Zeel didn't think had ever visited.

However, having said yes to him, she agreed. By the time they'd solidified their plans, it was time for them to leave.

Leaning in for a quick kiss before leaving the library, Advait turned to her and said, "It's a date Ms. Kapoor. Don't keep me waiting."

Date. That word sent shivers of excitement down Zeel's spine. She had never been on a date before. She didn't know what to expect, but she knew she was very excited to find out!

***

Next station MG Road. Agla Station MG Road. The doors will open to the right. Darwaze daayein taraf khulenge.

Zeel opted to abandon her car in favour of taking the metro for her date. Clad in jeans and a charming yellow top borrowed from her friend Madiha, who had assisted her in getting ready, Zeel wasn't entirely certain about her outfit choice for the date. However, considering the location was in a less formal part of town, she opted for simplicity. Sporting her branded white sneakers, she added a necklace adorned with small golden stars. Not one to indulge much in makeup, she decided on a touch of gloss and a hint of eyeliner to complete her look. For Zeel, who typically didn't pay much attention to dressing up, this experience felt like uncharted territory. Nevertheless, like everything else in life, she was eager to explore this new side of herself.

Upon leaving home, Zeel earned a raised eyebrow from Zeshan. Crafting a vague excuse about attending a slam poetry event with Madiha, she left home with a sense of confidence. However, as the metro approached her destination, she felt butterflies fluttering in the pit of her stomach. The mix of excitement and nervousness was palpable as she realized she was stepping into unfamiliar but thrilling territory.

Stepping out of the station, Zeel was a a little tentative. Not only was the area unfamiliar to her, it was also a place which housed several slums. Unsure of what to expect, she decided to wait for Advait at the designated meeting place. She didn't have to wait too long though for she spotted Advait soon enough. He was walking towards her, his usual sense of confidence intact. However, what she wasn't expecting was the person who was with him, for right next to him was none other than Saloni. Zeel could feel the excitement she had felt earlier flicker a little bit inside her. Maybe she had heard wrong when Advait had said this was a date. However, she didn't really know what to expect, so she pasted a fake smile on her face when she saw them both approach her.

"Hey," said Advait softly when he saw her.

"Hi," she said, a bit shyly.

To her credit, Saloni looked just as surprised to see Zeel and she was to see Saloni. "Hi Saloni," she added.

"Hi," she said, her face unsmiling. "What's she doing here Chitre? I thought you said we had a lot to do today. I didn't know we were going to be babysitting this little girl."

Zeel was taken aback at the blatant animosity that was dripping from Saloni. But not one to back down, she said, "I was invited. Advait invited me."

"Ladies, ladies. Relax," turning to Saloni he said, "I did invite her. I want her to meet the guys." Then turning to Zeel he said, "Ignore Saloni. She's not had her coffee yet. She's usually crabby until she gets her caffeine fix."

Saloni made a face but didn't push the topic any further. The three of them set off at a brisk pace with Saloni leading the way.

"Where exactly are we going?" asked Zeel.

"You'll see soon enough. Just promise me, you'll keep an open mind," said Advait.

Zeel's concern grew as events unfolded. Encountering Saloni had unsettled her, and the uncertainty about the situation had only intensified. Despite her initial hesitations, she chose to place her trust in Advait, deciding to follow the girl down a narrow dirt road that seemed to lead directly into the heart of the nearest slum.

Having lived in the city, Zeel had often encountered homeless people, especially at traffic signals, and seen street urchins peddling trinkets on street corners. However, this marked her first venture into a slum. The stark reality of abject poverty struck her, witnessing people living without access to basic necessities. What truly tugged at her emotions were the conditions of the young children—half-naked and unwashed yet finding contentment in playing with broken toys salvaged from the trash. The sight moved her, evoking a deep sense of empathy and a desire to make a difference.

She wasn't entirely sure why Advait had decided to bring her to this place, but it was about to become apparent to her soon. Saloni came to an abrupt halt outside what looked like an old warehouse. Zeel could hear some weird sounds coming from the inside but couldn't really make out the source since the place looked rather dark from the outside.

Saloni stepped into the warehouse without bothering to turn around. But Advait offered Zeel his hand which she gladly took. Of all the things Zeel had expected to find inside the warehouse, a bunch of kids from the slums huddled together over what looked like musical instruments was not something Zeel had anticipated.

"Welcome to our little jam session Zeel," said Advait with a proud smile on his face.

Saloni, who barely smiled was happily hi-fiving the kids as they all began setting up their various instruments.

Zeel was speechless. Advait took her over to where the kids were and started introducing each one of them to her.

"This is Pintya, Bunty, Raju, Mala, Dipti and that one over there messing with the harmonica is Vicky." At first sight, Zeel thought they were all about 8-10 years old, but the youngest one was actually 12 and the oldest being 16. Lack of proper nutrition clearly had affected their growth, making them look younger and thinner than they ought to be. However, the twinkle in their eyes was intact, and Zeel realised it was partly because of what Advait and Saloni had been working on with them.

"Hi guys!" said Zeel, genuinely excited to meet the kids who looked super happy to be there.

They all seemed very familiar with both Saloni and Advait and one of them (was it Bunty?) who good naturedly started teasing Advait about bringing his *cchhavi* (date) to their jam session.

"*E gapp bas re! Palun jaayel ti!* (Shut up or she'll run away!)" said Advait. Zeel didn't understand a lot of Marathi but she definitely got the gist for the kids started laughing while continuing to tease Advait. Saloni didn't seem to pleased about it all, but Zeel didn't really care.

"*Chala chala, suru karuya* (Come on, let's begin)," said Saloni, hurrying the kids along.

Advait improvised a makeshift seat for their sole audience member, Zeel, by turning an old crate upside down. In no time, the children positioned themselves, and Advait joined them on the drums.

With a synchronized start at Advait's cue, the ragtag band of kids began playing their instruments. While Saloni, the only non-musician besides Zeel, documented the entire performance, Zeel was captivated by the children's musical prowess. Her heart skipped a beat each time she caught Advait's gaze; his hazel eyes remained fixed on her throughout the entire performance. However, what truly moved Zeel was the realization that the kids weren't just playing any music—they were performing tunes she knew all too well. They were songs from her mother's hit films of bygone years.

As the kids approached the end of their final song, Zeel became aware of the moisture on her cheeks. Overwhelmed with sheer happiness, she had been shedding tears throughout the performance. As the performance drew to a close, Zeel burst into heartfelt applause, enthusiastically joining the children who were celebrating with a little jig. Letting go of any inhibitions, she took a leap forward and embraced Advait, who was already waiting with open arms. Without a second thought, she pressed her lips to his.

Advait, who was also caught by surprise, took a moment to right himself but soon surrendered to the kiss as well. Both were lost in a moment of intimacy right there in the midst of kids going 'whoa' and teasing Advait even more. The only person who didn't seem very pleased was Saloni who refused to even look in their direction and was busy tinkering with her phone.

It was only then the general chatter of the kids around them became louder, that Zeel realised what she had done. She turned beet red and tried to busy her face in Advait's chest who was only too happy to oblige. Her little moment of panic was too cute for words, and he absolutely adored Zeel in that very moment. Slowly recovering from her temporary lapse of judgment, Zeel finally made eye contact with him and was delighted to see pure joy reflected in them.

"Thank you," he said.

"Why are you thanking me? I should be the one thanking you!" protested Zeel.

"Thank you for coming here, for trusting me. I hope you liked our performance. The kids worked very hard to make they learned all the music in time for this," said Advait.

"Wait, they just started learning music?" asked Zeel.

"Not really. We've been practicing for a few months now, but these songs were new to them," he said.

"Did you…did you get them to learn these songs for me?" Zeel couldn't believe it!

"Zeel, I know you love your mom and how heartbroken you were that day when the scandal broke. I just wanted to make you smile," he said, still holding her close.

"Advait, when did you even manage to do all of this?" she was genuinely surprised.

"Well, the day after you were mobbed by the journalists…" he trailed off as he noticed realization dawning on Zeel's face. He had missed her small media statement inviting him to be her friend, as he was occupied with something far more crucial, all for her.

"You're insane. Oh my god, you're completely crazy!" Zeel exclaimed, a mix of laughter and tears in her voice.

"Zeel, I told you. You had me at that first annoyed look you gave me at orientation. I was a goner right then and there," said Advait.

"Then why didn't you ask me out earlier?" asked Zeel.

"Would you have said yes?" he asked in all seriousness.

"Probably not," said Zeel, nodding her head in understanding.

"So, now that you've seen our little performance, what's your review?" asked Advait, lightening the moment.

"My review?" turning to the kids, Zeel said, "This was by far the best thing I've witness all year! It was absolutely fantastic! You guys are such rockstars. Thank you so much, guys. This was truly amazing."

Turning to Saloni, Zeel asked, "Saloni, could I have a copy of the video you've taken? I'd like to keep visiting it whenever possible."

"It'll be going up on their social media handles soon. You can check it there," came her curt reply.

"Come on Saloni, just give her the video," said Advait.

"Fine. Give me your phone. It's a heavy file. It might take a moment," said Saloni.

Totally caught up in her happy moment, Zeel unlocked her phone and handed it to Saloni, asking her to transfer the video. She couldn't wait to watch it over and over again, relishing the wonderful feeling she had in that moment.

***

Chapter 12

Zeel's spirits soared after an entire day filled with laughter, kids, and Advait. Saloni had left right after the performance, instantly lifting Zeel's mood. Even though there might not have been any romantic connection between Saloni and Advait, Zeel couldn't shake the image of the girl sticking close to him. To make matters worse, Saloni kept shooting Zeel nasty looks that only added to the romantic tension in the air.

Following a quick round of pizzas and cupcakes which the kids polished off within seconds, Advait leaned over to Zeel and whispered in her ear, "Ready for the date?"

Zeel was under the impression that meeting the kids was the date, which must have showed on her face because Advait laughed quietly and added, "You didn't think this was the date I was referring to?"

The blush that spread on Zeel's lit up Advait's face as well. "Let's go?" Zeel took his waiting hand as he led her behind the warehouse where he had parked his bike.

"Where are you taking me now?" Asked Zeel.

"Always so curious! Have a little patience and you'll find out soon," he said with a wink.

"I'm not big on surprises," said Zeel.

"Hey, I didn't see you complaining earlier today!" he countered.

It was true, wasn't it? She had loved the surprise he had planned for her. "So, what say? Still want to know or are you willing to open your mind to new possibilities?" he asked, clearly teasing her.

Rolling her eyes, she said, "Fine! Lead me, Mr. Chitre."

***

Riding pillion with Advait was exhilarating. While the boy had made sure he was carrying an extra helmet for Zeel, he rode his motorcycle like a pro. Deftly winding in and out of the tiny back lanes of the city, Advait made sure Zeel held on to him tight.

In less than half an hour, they pulled up to a nondescript looking building which seemed to house nothing significant, let alone a place for a first date. Parking just under the building, Advait held out his hand once again for Zeel to guide her to the old elevator that stood at the end of the building lobby. It was one of those old school elevators that had those scissor gates made of grills that one had to manually slide open and shut.

After ensuring she was securely inside the elevator, Advait slid the grill shut and pressed the button for the top floor. The whirring of turning cogs was somewhat muffled by the scratchy elevator music. Abruptly, the elevator came to a halt.

From the way the building had looked on the outside, Zeel was certain there was nothing besides a few offices housed within. However, she was pleasantly surprised to see a cute little space where the elevator had deposited them. Right opposite to where they stood was a door which led to a place called 'The Book and The Bean'. Advait gestured for her to move forward, and even opened the door for her.

Zeel found herself captivated by the enchanting scene before her. 'The Book and The Bean' stood out as the most charming cafe she had ever set foot in. Perched atop the building, this cozy terrace cafe boasted a library adorned with the comfiest couches and chairs scattered about. Everywhere her eyes wandered, plants dangled from bookshelves or nestled into whimsical little pots in charming nooks. The ambiance was further enhanced by twinkling lights and colourful lampshades, creating the most delightful reading spaces. Judging by the enticing aroma wafting through the air, Zeel was confident that the coffee they brewed here would be nothing short of magical.

"What is this place? And how do I not know of its existence!" she exclaimed.

"Do you like it?" he asked.

"Like it? I love it. This place is beautiful! How did you find out about it?" she asked.

"Actually, it was just by chance. I had had a bad fight at home and had taken my bike out to ride my anger off, and that's when I spotted a small sign near this building. I decided to check it out and it's been my haunt ever since," he said earnestly.

"So, do you bring all your dates here?" asked Zeel, avoiding his eyes.

"Not all. Just the special ones," he responded. Zeel tried to hide her disappointment but failed.

Thankfully, Advait decided not to tease her any longer and said, "The only other 'date' I've brought here was my dad. He's an author and is also the reason behind my love for books and reading. I just had to share this place with him. However as far as girls are concerned, you're the first and only one."

Zeel punched his arm playfully. How he could be so annoying and so loveable at the same time was beyond her.

Seeing her smile return, he continued, "I find solace here whenever I need a bit of peace in my life. Plus, the owner of this cafe is one of the coolest people I know. Needless to say, he and my dad have become great friends, often spending hours engaged in lively political debates!"

He steered her towards a particular corner which seemed to be his favourite. Just as they were settling down, Zeel asked, "And your mom?"

"What about my mom?" said Advait blankly.

"You both seem to have a rather difficult relationship," she said softly, tentative about how he would react.

"You noticed, huh?" he said feigning surprise.

Zeel made a face.

Letting out a sigh, he said, "I love my mom. I really do. But there are times when I just cannot understand how one of the most intelligent and loveable people, I know can be completely obtuse."

When Zeel didn't say anything, he continued, "I was very close to mom. I was pretty much the idea child. Being a middle kid, you either turn out to be a total jerk or a total people pleaser. I was the latter. I lived for my mom's approval. She was loving yes, but she also tends to be extremely hard on all of us. However, Atharva, my older brother is her blue-eyed-boy - the one who can never do anything wrong. And the annoying thing is, I believe that too. He's unbelievably good and obedient, it's annoying. I really hope he gets his chance with the Indian cricket team this year. He's extremely good and I know he has it in him to become the next big sport star of the country."

Zeel smiled at the genuine fondness he seemed to have for his brother. With her encouragement, he continued, "Anuya my sister, on the other hand, is the baby of the house and a total *papa ki pari* (daddy's girl). But even she's a star. She's been learning Indian classical music since she was a baby and is a very good singer. And I love her to bits!"

"That leaves the little old me. I worked extra hard to be good, studied longer hours, practiced for chess tournaments during every vacation, did everything by the book. Drumming ws the only thing that I felt was truly mine - the one thing I will forever be grateful to my dad for who insisted on me doing it despite the fact that my mom hates it! Initially I didn't want to take up drumming because it would upset my mom. But then I realised how much I loved it. However, I would always have to work doubly hard at school to earn the privilege of playing the drums. But somehow, I always fell short. Sure, I won a few chess championships, scored decent enough marks and all that but I was never the best. I was always somewhere at the top, but never the topper. Never the No. 1 guy. I was always just good, never great. So I never questioned the path that was chosen for me and was set on joining engineering. Even got accepted into some good engineering colleges," he said.

Zeel was a good listener and Advait somehow felt very comfortable opening up to her.

He continued, "But then, everything changed. Right before starting engineering college, I decided to go on a biking trip with some buddies. It was the first time ever I was exploring the world that was beyond my comfort zone. And what I saw, had a deep impact on me. I would always make fun of all these Hollywood movies where the protagonists would come to India to 'find themselves.' But the thing was, I didn't realise how badly I needed to do it too."

"Zeel, we live in great luxury in our cities and lead such insanely privileged lives! And yet, we're so unhappy. I met people on that trip. Simple people who had very little and yet so much to give and so much to share. And I met kids who had nothing. One of those kids actually robbed me, you know. We had set up camp close to a village and the next day I woke up to find everything I had carried with me missing! But you know what was funny?" he asked.

Zeel raised her eyebrows in question.

"I didn't care one bit. I didn't care that my wallet was gone and that my phone was gone. I had earned so much on that one trip that it had completely turned my head. Also, I think it was probably the effect of the blunt I had smoked the night before," he said, winking, "Yeah, by the way the cigarette you caught me smoking, was actually a joint."

"What?" Zeel exclaimed. Advait laughed quietly at her absolutely horrified expression.

"You're such a sweet girl Zeel. Never change okay?" he said, pinching her cheeks.

"But anyway, the thing was, that I got back from the trip, and I no longer wanted to study engineering. I didn't want to spend four years studying something I did not enjoy. And then I didn't want to leave all that behind and do an MBA to get into some MNC and earn a fat salary. The thought of the future that I had once believed to be the only path forward was now more terrifying than ever. So, I sat my parents down and told them I didn't want to study engineering." he said.

"Oh! I can imagine how that went," said Zeel.

"Dad was pretty cool about it. He's an author. The man understands the importance of passion and creativity. Mom was livid. She couldn't understand how I could throw my career away this way. My bother has also studied law, you know. And he would have become a lawyer had he not been chosen for the Under 19 World Cup cricket team. My sister, she's currently in junior college, but she loves science and will most likely end up becoming a physicist or something. So, I was supposed to be the engineer. And I kicked all that away to follow my dreams! And that doesn't sit well with my mom." he said in a resigned tone.

"So, what is the dream?" asked Zeel.

"I want to help people. The reason I took up sociology as my key subject was because I genuinely want to help people. In fact, I've also lined up an internship with an organization that's working towards rural development in India. But yeah, I also want to be a professional drummer. I'd love to be a part of a band. I want to help the kids I hang out with. That's why I started a social media video channel for them. We upload our little jam sessions. I get musician friends to come and teach them. We also play gigs, you know?…There's so much I want to do…" he trailed off and seemed to be lost in thought.

"Does your mom know all this?" Asked Zeel.

"Nope. We stopped communicating a long time ago. My dad knows and loves what I'm doing. I asked him not to tell mom. If she could not support and understand me when I needed it the most, I don't care about her support now," he said, his voice cracking just a little bit.

Zeel took his hands in her own and said, "I get it. Our families may be as different as chalk and cheese, but the pressure is the same. I am expected to get over my obsession with pursuing psychology and train to become an actor. It's not my thing. I'm just not the one who likes to be in front of the cameras. That's my brother's dream. He loves it, and I support his dream a 100 per cent! My sister also did not want to be in the public eye, and she rebelled which only landed her in trouble. So, I get it. I understand the pressure you must be feeling. But in my case, I guess, it pays to have a dysfunctional family because at least it means they're not constantly on my case."

She gave him a little sad smile.

"Okay…enough of this. I'd much rather focus on happy things right now than discussing my mom or how we're letting our parents down…" said Advait in an attempt to change the topic.

Laughing, Zeel agreed wholeheartedly.

"So why don't you tell me what's good here, Mr. Chitre? I'm sure you have a favourite drink," asked Zeel.

"You bet!" came a quick response accompanied by a big smile that lit up his eyes.

***

Chapter 13

Zeel woke up with the sweetest smile on her face. The media frenzy around her was also losing steam when the media realised there wasn't much that was going to happen with Zeel and both Zeshan and Jigna had done a good job of keeping their mother out of trouble. Zeel also realised that her father had probably been stepped in to keep Kanika from making stupid comments in the media as well.

Regaining a sense of normalcy, Zeel found herself caught up in relishing the newfound calm. It was the weekend, and she was lazing in her bed. She had plans with Advait later in the day, but right now, she was devouring a new fantasy book she had been eager to sink her teeth into for weeks!

She was on a particularly exciting chapter when she suddenly heard a loud Zeshan let out a loud expletive from the room next door. Zeel was used to her twin's unnecessarily dramatic manner of reacting to everything. He had probably misplaced a sock or something. Without giving it another thought she continued with her book, when suddenly her brother burst into the room, with, "What the hell Zeel! When were you going to tell me?"

Caught off-guard, Zeel dropped her book to look at her brother who looked livid for some reason. "What happened? Why are you screaming?" asked Zeel.

"Zeel, why on earth is there a video of you kissing Advait circulating online?" Zeshan's words made her stop in her tracks.

"What are you talking about?" Zeel grabbed the phone from Zeshan's hands and hit play. On the screen was a video from the jam session with the kids. While the entire performance was on screen, so was the part where Zeel had leaped forward to kiss Advait. The angle from which the video was shot made the sweet kiss seem like something much nastier and the fact that it was done in front of kids made it seem even worse. However, what truly made Zeel's stomach turn were the comments on the video...

Is that Zeel Kapoor? The Kapoor women are something else, aren't they? Fist Zinnia, then the mother and now this one!

Friendship, my foot. They're clearly banging!

DFAQ. NGL, he's a snack. But she's so basic.

Come kiss me Zeel, I'll be your friend too *kiss emoji* *kiss emoji*

Seeing her moment of innocent abandon being put on display for the world to gawk at and make fun of made the colour drain from Zeel's face. She didn't even bother to check the news. It had been a couple of hours since the video had been up. By now every news out from Kashmir to Kanyakumari and beyond would have probably covered the news.

The sudden ringing of the phone almost made her drop it to the floor. Zeshan snatched it from her to answer it.

"Yeah Jigna..."

"You saw it..."

"I know but this is not what we planned...

"Can we get it pulled down?"

"No Jigna..."

"Whatever, handle this…."

"This is not how we wanted it!"

Zeel could barely make out what her brother was saying into the phone. She could feel her vision blurring and her body going numb and cold.

"Zeel! Zeel!"

Zeel didn't know what had happened, but suddenly she saw Zeshan, Jigna, Madiha and her mom standing over her trying to shake her as she lay on the floor in a foetal position. How she had reached there, she had no idea.

"Zee, baby, are you okay?" asked her mother who finally seemed to have emerge from her own daze.

"Mummy!" cried Zeel, "What happened?"

"Nothing happened baby girl. Are you okay?" Asked her mom.

"Yes…No," said Zeel. She could feel tears running down her cheeks as she said it. Just then her phone started ringing. It was Advait.

Before she could answer it, Zeshan grabbed it away from her.

"You asshole! You made big show of wanting to be my sister's friend and then you do this to her? How dare you upload such a video of hers?" Zeel wanted to talk to Advait. She knew Advait would never do something like that to her, but before she could say anything Zeshan walked out with the phone saying, "Don't you dare set your foot here…"

Within moments, the doorbell rang which was followed by a "You bastard…" from Zeshan and the sound of someone being hit.

Zeel, accompanied by her mom, Madiha and Jigna, hurriedly emerged to witness Zeshan preparing to strike Advait once again, having already drawn blood from a previous hit to his face. Taking note of what was happening, both Madiha and Zeel jumped into action. Zeel went straight to check on Advait while Madiha tried to restrain Zeshan.

"Get out of my way Madiha. I'm going to kill this guy!" Zeshan was clearly seeing red.

"Stop it, Zishu!" pleaded Zeel. "Are you okay?" She asked Advait who gave her a quick nod.

"Zeshan let him go. I don't think he's done it. He wouldn't have been here otherwise," Madiha tried to reason with him.

"Madiha, stay out of this. This guy was bad news from day one!" said Zeshan, still itching to hit Advait.

"Stop it! Stop all this now!" Screamed Zeel. Turning towards Advait, she said, "It was Saloni, wasn't it?"

"I think so. She shows me another edit of the video asking me if she could upload it to the channel. I said yes. I didn't bother to check the video once it had gone up on the site. It was only when one of the kids contacted me to tell me about it is when I came straight to you. I'm sorry, baby. I don't know what happened. But I'm going to get to the bottom of it." said Advait, holding Zeel close.

"I'll go with you," said Zeel.

"You're not going anywhere with him Zeel!" growled Zeshan.

"Let her be Zeshan. She's not a child." yelled Madiha.

Adhira, for her part had taken the moment to get some ice for Advait's face. "Are you okay son?" she asked quietly.

"Yes ma'am. Please believe me, I love Zeel. I'd never hurt her this way," he said.

Love. Advait loved her. All this while Zeel was unsure about the depth of Advait's feelings for her, always wondering whether there was someone else, someone better he could go for. And all this while, he had slowly been falling in love with her? So badly she wanted to hold him and scream those three words back at him. But now was not the right time. Not with Zeshan still foaming at the mouth and Jigna glued to her phone trying to do damage control.

Advait's words which were like music to Zeel's ears only proved to fuel Zeshan's anger some more.

Madiha who was still holding on to Zeshan said, "You heard him, Zeshan. Let it go! They're in love."

"Love, my foot. Madiha, you don't know anything about love. You're a fool if you think people actually fall in love. It's lust! I know how guys think. I am a guy. I see a hot chick and I don't think I'm in love. I'm thinking of how to get into her pants. You think I don't know about your little crush on me? I'm not blind Madiha. But I never acted on it because you're in some fantasy world where you think we will fall in love and get married and have babies. I'm not that guy, and guess what, neither are most guys. So spare me all this romantic crap you're so into and grow up," spat Zeshan.

His words felt like a slap to her face. Madiha let go of his hand. Her vision grew blurry with the tears that had suddenly gathered at the corners of her eyes. She pushed past Advait and Zeel and stormed out of their house.

"Zeshan!" screamed Zeel, "What is wrong with you?"

Zeel was torn between staying with Advait and running after her friend. Finally, she grabbed his hand and decided to leave. Madiha was more than just a friend. And Advait did not hesitate even for a moment.

"Zeshan that was completely uncalled for. Why did you do that to the poor girl?" said Adhira.

"What? I'm said only what's true. Look at you, the love fool that you've been? What did you get out of it? And you expect me to believe in love! Hah!" Zeshan let out a sarcastic laugh.

"You can laugh all you want my son, but some day you're going to regret what you've said today," said Adhira whose heart was breaking for both her kids. She had never intended for the lack of love in her own life to become a curse for her kids. But that's what had happened and now they were all dealing with the devastating consequences.

***

"Madiha, wait!" screamed Zeel. "Stop!"

Madiha only quickened her pace. She was clearly crying. Finally, Zeel caught up with her with Advait in tow.

"Hey babe, please don't cry," Zeel ran up to her friend and pulled her into a hug.

"You always told me he was an ass. I guess I just had to experience it myself," said Madiha.

"Babe, please. Please don't pay attention to what he said. You know how he is. When he's angry and hurting he lashes out at others," said Zeel. She knew her brother had messed up horribly, but she also loved him dearly and understood he probably hadn't meant a word of what he had said.

"Hey Madiha, I know I'm practically a stranger to you, but please don't let Zeshan's words affect you. I could see what he said wasn't the truth. I've seen you guys around college. He cares about you. I know that. Please, please don't let this hurt you. He was angry with me, and he shouldn't have but he took it out on you. You just got caught in the crosshairs. You need to know it wasn't about you," said Advait.

Madiha looked at him and back and Zeel, "Thanks guys. And I'm sorry Zeel. I know you guys have a bigger crisis to deal with. I don't want you both to worry about me. I'll be fine. I think whatever he said, was for the best. At least I won't be pining over him anymore. You guys should go figure out this video mess. I'll head home. Zeel, call me. I'm always there for you."

With that, Madiha got into the car and asked her driver to move on.

Zeel's heart broke for her best friend. Madiha didn't deserve this. Not at all. She was never going to be able to forgive Zeshan for what he had done to her friend.

Turning to Advait she said, "I'm sorry about this whole thing." On seeing the blooming black eye on Advait's face, she asked him, "How are you feeling? Is your face hurting?"

"I'll be fine. Don't worry about me. Are you okay?" he asked quietly.

"No. Not really. Everything is a mess, and I don't know where to begin. Maybe it's time we find out why Saloni would do something like that!" said Zeel.

"Let's go," said Advait gesturing her towards him bike.

***

Chapter 14

"Open up Saloni! I know you're in there," screamed Advait while banging on her door.

Saloni lived with roommates. One of her roommates had let Zeel and Advait into the house. They were currently banging on her bedroom door.

After almost ten minutes of banging, Saloni finally opened her door with a, "What?"

"Why the hell did you do that Saloni?!" demanded Advait, "Why did you upload the wrong video?"

Saloni looked at his face and started laughing, the sound grating on Zeel's nerves.

"The wrong video? Oh baby! It was the right video," said Saloni with a sly smile.

"Saloni! Do you have any idea what you've done? The shitstorm that you've unleashed?" asked Advait.

"You think this video and what the media is saying about it is a shitstorm? The you're naiver than I thought you were," she said.

"What the hell do you mean by that?" he asked, a little confused.

"Why don't you ask your little girlfriend here?" said Saloni.

Now even Zeel looked confused.

"Quit playing games Saloni. Delete that bloody video and tell us why did you do it?" said Advait.

"I'm not deleting anything. I didn't do anything wrong. She chose to kiss you. She chose to pounce on you without thinking. She should have known better. But then again, what else can I expect from a Bollywood kid? All these girls they claim to be all innocent but they're all the same," said Saloni. Turning towards Zeel, she said, "You could have had any guy. Any guy in the entire college. Hell, in the entire city. But no. You had to trap the one boy I wanted!"

"What?!" spat Advait. "What crap is this?"

"Why did you never notice me Advait? Why do you think I broke up with my loser ex-boyfriend? He was nothing in front of you. When we started working together making videos, I realised you were the one I wanted, not him! That day in the library, I wanted to kiss you for real, but then this bitch had to show up to ruin it all. I wasn't going to let that go. I had to do something. I was waiting for an opportunity. Adn guess what? You brought it straight to me. I didn't have to do a thing. You did it to yourself, Zeel. So, spare me the victim act, because we know you're no better than me."

"Saloni, just stop! Is this your way of showing you want to be with me? What's all this nonsense? I can't be with someone so deceitful! You are a liar and a cheat and all you've done is hurt me and hurt Zeel," yelled Advait.

Zeel knew the moment she had seen the video that she was right about her initial assessment of Saloni. She knew Saloni wanted Advait. She just did not know how badly. Guess she knew now.

"Advait, you really think Zeel is any different from me? What? Is it her pretty doe like eyes? Or the righteousness she oozes from every pore of her body? Is that what you fell for? What if I told you Zeel was exactly like me!" said Saloni.

"What the hell does that mean?" asked Advait, fed up with Saloni's lies.

"Why don't you ask your little girlfriend about her journal entries?" said Saloni with a triumphant look on her face.

The instant those words escaped Saloni's lips; Zeel sensed a hollow emptiness gnawing at the pit of her stomach.

"What are you talking about? What journal entries? Stop spewing more lies to save yourself," said Advait.

"Ask her!" yelled Saloni. "Actually, you know what, let me show you!" She yanked the phone out of Zeel's hands and unlocked it. Zeel remembered unlocking the phone in front of her back at the warehouse and cursed herself for it. "Here - see this! And then tell me who's a liar and a cheat!"

Saloni shoved the phone in Advait's face. He grabbed it from her to take proper look.

"Advait…" Zeel, who had been eerily quiet so far, finally spoke up.

"Advait, listen to me…"

Advait fell into an eerie silence. He scrolled through the entire plan that Jigna and Zeshan had crafted for Zeel, absorbing every detail meticulously outlined. There it was, the entire scheme, presented in a sequence. He couldn't help but notice the minor tasks Zeel had marked as completed, even though events hadn't unfolded in the chronological order initially intended. The friendship, the kiss, the date...there was so much more in there. He found it difficult to take in. To breathe.

"Zeel?" he didn't even have to ask the question. He had already seen the guilt in Zeel's eyes. His fear confirmed, "Why Zeel?"

"I told you she was a liar!" Saloni tried to pipe in but one withering look from Advait made her zip her mouth shut.

"Advait, I can explain," said Zeel, completely unsure of how she was going to do it.

"I'm waiting to hear it. Tell me. What the hell is this, Zeel?" Zeel could see the anger rising in him.

"Advait, it wasn't supposed to be this way. You know how we started out. After my mom's scandal flared up in the media and you stepped in to help me out…our publicist thought it would be a good idea if the media actually saw us as a couple. That it would take the attention away from my mom's scandal…" began Zeel.

"So, you just went along with the idea… because playing with someone's feelings isn't wrong in your books, is it, Ms. Kapoor?" he asked sarcastically.

"That's not the case Advait. You know I love you," said Zeel.

"Please don't Zeel. Please do not disrespect love this way. Wow. First your brother and now you. Today's been a day of revelations," said Advait, shaking his head.

A soft sob slipped from Zeel. "I'm sorry, Advait. Please don't be this way."

Ignoring her pleas, Advait asked, "Zeel, was anything true? I trusted you. I showed you my heart. I told you things I've never told anyone. Was anything you said true?"

"It was all true Advait. Every single bit. You know it!" Pleaded Zeel.

"How do I know, Zeel? Right now, all I can see are tick marks on an app. I'm nothing but a to-do-list to you," the dejection in his voice was more than Zeel could bear.

She held his face with both her hands, "Look at me Advait, please. I know it's all messed up but trust me, every single thing we shared we a hundred per cent true. I love you Advait. I really do. You have no idea what you mean to me. You've made me feel alive in ways I never knew possible. You showed me how to look at the world differently…."

Advait abruptly pulled away from Zeel, "I have to go. I…"

"Advait, no! Please listen to me…" cried Zeel.

"I need to think Zeel. And I can't do that here. Not when you're around. I can't think straight when I am around you. I have to go. I'm sure you can call Zeshan to pick you up, or whatever." With that, Advait turned around and walked out of the room and out of Zeel's life.

***

Chapter 15

It had been two weeks since Zeel had last seen Advait. He had not answered a single text of hers and had disconnected his phone. The media had played their video of kissing each other on loop for three whole days before abandoning it in favour of news about a TV actor who was caught cheating on his pregnant wife with none other than her best friend.

Night after night, Zeel had wept into her pillow, and each day at college, she anxiously scanned the classroom, hoping for Advait's entrance that never happened. She could sense the whispers and gossip from her classmates behind her back. However, only Saloni and Madiha knew the complete story. After the ordeal, Zeel had confided in Madiha about the plan and the journal app. "Oh, Zeel!" Madiha hugged her friend, understanding that Zeel could never deceive someone in such a manner.

While she was truly thankful to have Madiha by her side, she knew her best friend was dealing with her own pain inflicted upon her by Zeel's brother. Zeel couldn't help but think back to the first day of college when everything felt so right. How excited they were. How eager they were to take on the entire world. And now look where they were. Two broken girls trying to hold on to each other as their worlds fell spectacularly apart around them.

As the second week of being without Advait almost came to an end, Zeel couldn't take it anymore and decided to go ask the one person she thought might know if Advait was doing okay, if not his whereabouts.

"May I come in?" asked Zeel.

"How can I help you, Ms. Kapoor," asked Principal Manjiri Chitre.

"Principal Chitre, I just wanted to know if Advait is okay," asked Zeel, taking great effort to not break down in front of his mother.

"I don't know Ms. Kapoor. You tell me. I haven't seen my son since your little video hit the screens," said the older woman.

"What?!" said Zeel.

"Advait hasn't been home since that day. He called his father and told him he was going to be away for a few days." she said.

"Oh." That was the only thing Zeel could utter.

"Now if there's nothing else, Ms. Kapoor, please head back to your classes," said Principal Chitre.

Just as Zeel was about to leave, she stopped. She turned around to face Advait's mom.

"Don't you care about your son?" asked Zeel.

"Ms. Kapoor, this is not a conversation I want to have with you. Please leave." she said.

"Don't you care what's happened to him? Don't you want to know whether he is okay or not? In fact, when was the last time you even bothered to speak with him properly?" Zeel pressed on.

"Ms. Kapoor, you're overstepping your boundaries. Please do not presume to know what I feel or do not feel for my son." Principal Chitre was getting angry.

"Good. Then I'm glad I'm not speaking from assumptions. Your son loves you. He genuinely loves you. All he has ever wanted was your approval, and your love. Pure unconditional love. Love that isn't a result of some test he passed or some tournament he won. Do you know how hard he's working to make this world a better place in whatever little manner he can? I know you've seen the video and unfortunately people are focused on the least interesting thing in it. Did you see the joy he is bringing to the lives of those kids? What he is doing for them? How could you not love him for that?" said Zeel, her voice raised in anger.

"Who are you to question my love for my son?" asked Principal Chitre, who was more than a little irritate now.

"I am nobody. Or maybe I'm the girl your son poured his heart out to. And, well, I'm also the girl who shattered it," with that, Zeel's tears burst forth like a dam breaking.

"Ms. Ka…Zeel?" Principal Chitre's voice came in a soft whisper.

"I'm sorry. I just really am sorry. I didn't mean to hurt him, but I did. And don't know how to undo it!" Zeel had started shaking.

Principal Chitre pulled the sobbing Zeel into a motherly hug, "Shh..it's okay. I understand. Love isn't always easy."

Once her sobs subsided a little, Zeel righted herself, "I'm sorry Principal Chitre. I shouldn't have said all that I said to you. I just…I hurt him. On top of everything that he was already feeling. I was angry with myself and with the world. I shouldn't have lashed out at you this way."

Principal Chitre took a deep breath and asked Zeel, "Ms. Kapoor, do you know what is the true mark of a teacher?"

Zeel shook her head, unable to understand the relevance of the question.

"The true mark of a teacher is their perpetual commitment to learning. What you did today required courage, and I commend you for it. I also appreciate that you saw in my son what I never could - his passion. I watched the video; I witnessed his skill with the drum kit and how he connected with the kids, the pure joy on his face. As both a mother and a teacher, that's all I want for my children – for them to be happy. For the first time, I truly saw what brings joy to Advait. Moreover, I noticed something else – the smile you brought to his face. Zeel, I may not understand why things went wrong, but I know my son. When he loves, he loves with his entire being," said Advait's mom, wearing a sad smile.

Zeel nodded in acknowledgement, "Thank you."

"Don't worry about Advait. He needs time to get over whatever he is getting over. He will be back. I know that much about my son," she said with an encouraging smile.

Zeel replied with a tight smile, thanked her and left her office feeling considerably lighter than before. However, she had resolved to do something she never thought she would do.

Over the next few days, Zeel with Madiha in tow, made several trips to meet the kids she had seen performing and spent days hanging out with them. She made several public appearances with them in the media where she brought some of the kids from the video along with her, ensuring they got the media exposure they deserved. She made sure Jigna did whatever that was required to get these little musical prodigies whatever opportunities they could get.

Zeshan had let go of his anger, but his mom and sister were still giving him the cold shoulder. Madiha refused to even look in his general direction. He started hanging out a bunch with his buddy Raunak and helping his dad prep for the wedding. Oh yeah, by the way, Raghav and Kanika had set a wedding date. Zeel and Zeshan were worried about how it might affect their mom, but Adhira surprised everyone by going on her social media and sending love and luck to the engaged couple. This move left the media shocked, desperately searching for any bit of controversy. But Adhira was done with it all. She had decided to move on and was thinking about becoming a director. Right now, she was checking out scripts to find something to work on.

Things weren't perfect. But this would have to do. Zeel was still crying herself to sleep. She had just become better at hiding the pain from others.

***

"Anupam Sir, I know there's one box still left, I'll get to it soon… just need to finish this one bit…" said Zeel without looking up from the computer.

She had been spending her afternoons in the library, continuing with the task that was assigned to her and Advait. Madiha had started joining her on most days. Today, however, she was all by herself. She was almost done with cataloguing most of the books. There was just one last box left which would hardly take any time. So when she heard the door open, she didn't bother to look up, preferring to finish her work soon. Anyway, no one ever came to this back room that was assigned to them…besides Madiha and the librarian Anupam Sawant.

Which is why she was completely taken aback when she heard an all too familiar voice asking her, "Need a hand with the box?"

There, standing in front of her, was Advait. He looked exactly the same, except for a little bit of scruff around his jawline, which somehow made him look even more attractive.

Zeel sat there unable to say a word. She just stared at him. She was scared that if she blinked, he would probably disappear.

"Ms. Kapoor, I offered to help with that box," he repeated, his hazel eyes piercing into hers.

She nodded without saying a word. She saw him walk around to pick up the box and unpack it. She followed his every move keenly, still unsure about how to proceed.

"Thanks for looking out for the kids…" he said softly.

She nodded once again. Slowly finding her voice, she asked, "How're you?"

He just smiled in response.

"Where…were you?" she ventured.

"Around. Just clearing my head," he offered.

"Okay," she didn't know what else to say.

"I went to the coffee shop," she said eventually.

"I know. The owner told me," he said.

"I asked about you," she said.

"So, I heard," he kept moving the books around, laying them in neat piles.

You could cut the tension in the room with a knife.

"Advait."

"Zeel."

They both said at the same time. Their little synchronised act earned him a nervous laugh from Zeel.

"By the way, I also heard that you scolded my mother," said Advait, cocking an eyebrow in mock surprise.

Zeel snapped her head up in attention, exclaiming, "Oh my god! I didn't scold her, okay! I was just angry, and I didn't know who else to turn to. I didn't know what to do. Everything was wrong, and you weren't there. I really thought I would never see you again. Oh my god, this is so embarrassing!" Her cheeks flushed with red.

Her slightly nervous speech caused Advait to double over with laughter. Zeel felt extremely annoyed at how effortlessly he had managed to get under her skin, even when she was in no state to be irritated by him.

Walking over to her, Advait leaned in and cupped her face in his hands, "Zeel, I'm sorry."

"What are you sorry for? You didn't do anything wrong." said Zeel.

"But I did. I didn't believe you when you tried to tell me the truth. I'm sorry for being a jerk," he said, touching his forehead to hers.

"I'm sorry too Advait, I truly am. I never meant to hurt you. I was never going to carry out the plan. And the app, that was just me being me," said Zeel.

"I know. Only you could turn dating into a to-do-list," he teased her placing a tiny little kiss on her nose which was turning red with annoyance at what he had just said.

"Advait!" cried Zeel.

"Baby, I love you." said Advait.

"I love you, too," responded Zeel.

"I know. The last few weeks without you were hell. I don't care if you need up have an app to keep track of your dating life, I don't care if you need an entire entourage to help you with it! What I care about is…you. I'm sorry I went away this way. Just tell me I'm being a jerk next time I attempt anything like this, okay?" he asked.

Zeel nodded, her face breaking into her first genuine smile in weeks. Her Advait was finally back and with her. All she could think of was how her heart felt whole again. Standing on her tiptoes, she leaned in to kiss the boy she never thought she could ever get along with, let alone live without.

*** The End ***

Epilogue

"Yo, Zeshan, you coming?" asked Raunak.

"Yeah, I'll be right there, bro," said Zeshan, who was busy staring at his phone. In front of him was a picture his sister and her boyfriend Advait on a double date with Madiha and some guy. Zeshan couldn't stop staring at the arm that creep had put around Madiha's waist.

"Zeshan! We're going to be late!" said Raunak.

Zeshan's father was getting married, and Zeshan was going to be a witness in the civil ceremony. Both Zeel and his mothered had declined the invitation to attend the wedding, so Zeshan was on his own, that is if you didn't count Raunak who seemed to be the only person who spoke to him these days.

Putting the phone away Zeshan made his way to the car where Raunak was waiting for him, but not before shooting off a quick text to Jigna to find out more about the boy Madiha was dating. Not that he had a problem with her dating. He just wanted to make sure the guy she was dating wasn't going to hurt her in any way. That's the least he could do after the way he had treated her.

In retrospect, he realised what he had done, was probably for the best. He did not want to lead his sister's best friend on. It was easier to just rip of the band aid in one go. Also, he was already in talks with his father for launching him in the next movie. Things were finally going to according to plan.

Then why was he overcome with a feeling of emptiness and also a bit of rage on seeing that picture? He attempted to push the feeling away, but his thoughts were abruptly halted by the ringing of his phone. The caller ID displayed an unknown number.

"Zeshan, I didn't know who else to call. I need help," it was Madiha on the line.

The urgency in Madiha's voice echoed through Zeshan's ears, and suddenly, the weight of his own conflicted emotions paled in comparison to the gravity of her plea. As he answered her call, a chilling realization swept over him—his carefully planned life was about to take an unexpected turn.

But the question remained, was he ready to embark on this journey into the unknown? And what about Madiha? Would she be willing to look past what Zeshan had done to her?

Find out in the next book: THE PROBABILITY OF LOVE

***

www.ingramcontent.com/pod-product-compliance
Lightning Source LLC
Chambersburg PA
CBHW020610160726
47991CB00002BA/711